ABOUT THE BOOK

Werewolf Natalya Stravinsky might lose herself in a New Jersey shopping binge before she can get herself out of her this latest conundrum.

After uncovering the true thief for the demons at the ceramic mart, Nat should prop her feet up and take a long rest with her mate Thorn, but instead, a sleazy leprechaun strong-arms her into yet another task. Nat must buy five magical products for his pawn shop in a month or she'll end up as his indentured servant for good. Nat just wants to fulfill her side of the bargain and get out, but before she can do so, all hell breaks loose. The mystical merchandise she purchased begins to infect the supernatural marts in South Toms River, causing chaos and death among the customers.

Now, Nat must discover the culprit behind the tainted goods, or this quest could be her last.

LOWDOWN PAWN SHOP LEPRECHAUNS

A Flea Market Magic Novel

NEW YORK TIMES BESTSELLING AUTHOR

SHAWNTELLE MADISON

VALKYRIE
RISING
PRESS

CHAPTER ONE

I promised myself that someday—not today, mind you—
I'd figure out why folks tossed away their well-loved
trinkets, baubles, and doodads. Why give away your
beloved lawn chairs and questionable mattress sets when you
could give them to someone else? Instead of contributing to
the landfill problem, I stood in line at an estate sale to *help*.

The place in question, a bungalow north of South Toms
River, held few surprises. Most of the folks around here were
working-class, down-to-earth blue-collar humans. None of
them suspected they stood in line with two werewolves. My
mate Thorn and I were just like them, our hands full of the
abandoned Christmas cheer.

The late June morning couldn't have been more perfect.
Only a few stubborn, wispy clouds skirted across the sky and
a light breeze tugged at my husband's blond curls.

All was well until a lady holding an electric toothbrush
lined up behind us. I gave her the side-eye. Mouths had
billions of squirmy, nasty germs. Every single day someone
crammed that contaminated toothbrush into their mouth.
With a concealed frown, I edged away from her.

You can keep your petri dish on a stick, thanks.

As hard as I tried to keep my obsessive-compulsive disorder under control, some things scared the hell out of me.

"It's got Bluetooth and you can listen to your favorite songs while you brush," the lady gushed.

Yeah, still a hard pass.

Thorn chuckled, his lean face settling in a knowing grin. Like any caring spouse, he helped me carry my goodies. And not once did he ask if we needed these. *'Cause I believe we do.*

"Why are we so close to the Sourland Preserve again?" he asked instead.

I sighed. As hard as I tried to hypnotize myself into thinking everything was all right, I couldn't ignore the yipping chihuahua in the room.

"You already asked me that when we pulled up." I adjusted my purchases in my arms. "And when we left the house. And when you got on the Parkway."

The line shifted forward. "I asked because of what happened to you, Nat." His voice trailed off. He didn't need to elaborate.

Only twenty miles from where we stood, I'd faced off with two mighty foes. The first one arrived in the area two months ago and brought a torrent of dangerous and opportunistic mystical beings. The South Toms River nymphs referred to her as She Who Always Walks the Path, but I knew her true name: Diana the Huntress.

For millennia, Diana hunted along the Great Northern Fairy Path with her pack of beasts. Other creatures trailed after her seeking her power. My family had tangled with the Basilisk King. That horrible creature followed her around like a die-hard groupie.

I shivered. Not only did Diana take down my enemy, but she took me prisoner, too.

Thorn touched my shoulder. "The line is moving, babe." A flash of concern touched his features. He reached for the box of Christmas handkerchiefs in my hand. "Why don't you go to the SUV and I'll get these?"

"I'm fine." I squared my shoulders, but my mate had to smell my anxiety.

When I'd first seen the items for sale on an estate sale website, a delicious thrill coursed through me. The same feeling I always got when I glimpsed a rarity, a gem waiting to be plucked off a table. Who wouldn't drive a couple miles to snag a set of Victorian Christmas handkerchiefs?

Soon enough, we reached the cashier and I raced through the transaction. The summer breeze shifted and rustled the trees across the road. Kids frolicked around a sprinkler in the yard, unaware of the nearby supernatural threat. Somewhere north of here, the goddess waited for me. The collar she forced me to wear was gone, but I remembered the weight, the breathtaking pressure as it squeezed. I fumbled with numb fingers to stuff my credit card back into my purse. So far, I'd wrestled with this feeling, never mentioning Diana and pretending everything in South Toms River was well again.

"You smiled the whole way here. You okay?" he asked softly. "Maybe we shouldn't have come."

"Still gotta live my life." I shrugged. "I can't run away from her. There's no running away. Only waiting."

"Then let's go home. We'll get some burgers on the way."

"Sounds good to me. I have to deal with the leprechaun today."

That got a snarl from Thorn. While searching for a mystical whistle not too long ago, we'd run into a sleazy leprechaun pawn shop owner. To save the pack, I'd made another bargain: to get the whistle, I had to work with Seamus for one month to buy five items for his shop. When I made the bargain, I'd thought I was clever. I'd even added terms to protect myself like not buying anything lewd or alive. With my luck, Seamus wouldn't play fair.

"If he mysteriously disappears," Thorn said, "you won't have to work with him, will you?"

I laughed. "After a nuclear attack, he'd survive with the roaches. He isn't going anywhere."

As we returned to the SUV, I considered how many times I'd survived dangerous situations and somehow walked away. Those adversaries were nothing compared to Diana. I had a healthy fear of magic—especially of warlocks, wizards, and witches, but I didn't want to fathom what a goddess could do.

Not only to me, but to those I loved.

～

Traffic had picked up not long after I strode up to O'Malley's Pawn and Jewelry in Brooklyn. Usually I had a skip in my step when I approached a store, but my shoes scraped against the concrete. The door should've welcomed me with open arms and pulled me into the leprechaun's private domain. As much as I wanted to sate my shopaholic fix, the overpowering scent of Harvest Fresh Pine didn't quite cover the foul odors of unwashed clothing, rampant mold, and a stale pastrami sandwich.

I peered inside. A lone air conditioner rattled from its spot in a window. The machine blew warm air, heavy with a moldy scent. I sighed. By the end of the day, I'd have a nice colony of fungus growing on my backside.

At the far end of the narrow shop, tucked among the mishmash of goods in this establishment, Seamus smirked at me from behind his wall of bullet-resistant glass. My new employer for the month sported a reddish five o'clock shadow across his chin and ruddy cheeks. If I hadn't known how slimy he was, he might've been a cool guy to grab a drink with at the local pub.

"I'm mighty pleased to see you ready for work." Thanks to my goblin boss back in South Toms River, I could chop through the glamour hiding his true form. A man standing at waist-height smoothed back his ginger curls and gave me a leer-laden stare.

I had fifteen more minutes before my shift began, but whether I waited outside in the June heat or faced the leprechaun, I'd suffer somehow.

With a sigh, I shifted from resting on one hip to another.

"Can I start early?" I asked.

"Of course. Of course. I told Umbane to expect you this fine evening."

"And what does Umbane want to sell you?"

He cocked a half-grin. "You'll find out when you get there. His stock rotates once a month. With your sharp eyes, I know you'll pick out the best one."

"Do you have all five requests?" Might as well ask. "I don't have to work at The Bends tomorrow for Bill, so I thought I'd knock out all of them out tonight."

Seamus gave me a lazy grin. "Well, timing is important in our line of business. I could give you the list, but some of my associates are…"

I gestured for him to elaborate. "They're what?"

"A wee bit difficult to work with. Hence, why I hired you."

"Difficult as in they drive a hard bargain? Are they cheapskates? I can negotiate a better deal if I don't walk in blind."

"Bah! You're a clever lass. You go talk to Umbane first and let me know if you want another job." He reached down and grabbed something from behind the counter. The glass wall shimmered as he slid a burnt-orange T-shirt and piece of paper to me.

"Glad to have you working on Team Seamus," he said with a curt nod.

"Team Seamus, huh?" I drew up the too-small T-shirt and shuddered. "So you want me to put this on—as in I drape this filthy garment on my person?" I paused in case he was joking.

Not one of his employees, and I used that term loosely since they were likely his ladies of the evening, had to wear a tight T-shirt with the words, *"Nobody Does It Better Than Seamus."*

I could testify, after working for a leprechaun for the last three minutes, that anyone with a pulse could've done whatever *it* was much better than him.

"You're my first full-time employee," he said with his rough Irish burr. "When you're out and about buying my exclusive stock, you're representing my brand."

I tossed the shirt back on the counter. "You have a *brand?*"

A quick peek around me spoke volumes. Scuffs marred the wooden counter. Seamus's pine chair leaned to the side in distress and every single surface in this place had dust. "Are you aiming for the abandoned-store motif?"

"My brand made me enough cash to pay for the whistle you needed so badly."

Damn, he had a point there.

"Speaking of arrangements..." He leaned forward. "I already gave you the whistle as a part of our bargain. You said you'd take care of everything in a month. What you didn't specify was the consequence if you didn't hold up your end of the deal."

Shit. Shitty. Shit.

"I'll get everything done," I said firmly. According to the lewd calendar on the wall, I had to get all this done by July 28th.

"And if you don't? The way I see it, I gave you a priceless

product capable of summoning a hellhound. If you can't get me what I need, you'll have to pay the whistle's retail price."

"How much?"

He grabbed a filthy Post-it note with a grocery list including condoms. Nobody needed to know he wanted Silver Maximum Size. Eww. With a steady hand, he scribbled a number with five digits after it. With each zero he added, my stomach plummeted until I had to remind myself to breathe.

"That much, huh?" I murmured.

His grin oozed sliminess. "That's with the 'Seamus Employee Discount.' Either way, what's fair is fair. The way I see it, you can't afford to pay for the whistle. If you can't get me what I need, you should quit The Bends to pay your debt and the interest accrued."

"I'd become your new *gal* for how long?"

He didn't blink once. "Oh, forever sounds good."

CHAPTER TWO

According to the address Seamus had given me, I'd reached the right spot, a brightly lit shop right off the Parkway in Jersey. All around me, bleary-eyed humans commuted home while hints of the night life crept out. My day had just begun.

A white sign with the name *Electric Wing Lighting Co.* painted in gold told me I'd reached the right place. Darkness bathed the whole storefront. I stared through the double pane windows. Not a single customer graced the lighting store's aisles. I circled the entrance twice, sniffing for danger and any signs of magic. Underneath the pleasant aroma of dinner from a nearby Indian restaurant, I caught the unexpected bite of ozone. Almost as if a thunderstorm had passed recently.

I touched the doorknob and the hanging lights in front of the door flickered. Crimson light, like flames dancing to life, jumped from one bulb to another. The frenzy heightened with the crackle of sparks bouncing off the lighting merchandise. And when I mean merchandise, I mean every kind of fixture your little heart searched for.

A middle-aged, Black man with prominent cheekbones and a hint of a smile glanced at me from the other side of the store. He weaved around a display of bamboo lanterns to approach me.

"May I help you?" His voice brushed up against me like a stray cat, smooth yet affable.

"I'm one of Seamus's buyers. He told me you have products for me to pick up."

At the mention of the leprechaun's name, the man's beguiling features darkened. "I told him—last week no less—that I had no more thunder feathers."

He took a step toward me. A Moroccan lamp dimmed behind him. "Why does he keep pestering me?"

I twitched with alarm. Too often I'd learned bad things came in pretty packages.

Swallowing past my dry throat, I said, "Maybe we can make arrangements for later?"

The confident—yes, I should use that word—human in me stood her ground while the wolf nipped at my neck for me to retreat. I tried to quell my fast-beating heart and quickening breath, but I gasped instead. This man should be harmless, but I'd learned over the years that nothing in the supernatural world should be taken too lightly. An innocent-looking, old man could be taking a dragon for a walk. The sweet lady carrying her groceries to her car could be a witch preparing for a feast of five-year-olds.

And this creature was no man.

I blinked hard and focused. The glamour over the shopkeeper wavered.

The goblin blade strapped to my ankle pulsed in warning.

He grunted. "No so fast, Little Wolf. Just one bite before we conduct business."

Pain blossomed across my forehead as I pressed harder, plucking away at the spell. Behind the luxurious white shirt, black and golden feathers rustled. A snapping beak loomed above me. And whatever it was, it was far closer than it appeared.

Oh no. A lightning bird.

I growled and shuffled back a step. "I'm not edible."

He reached out and snatched my arm. My flesh flashed white as flames snaked up to my shoulder. But as my sleeve burned away, my skin never reddened or blackened. Back when I'd infiltrated my former demon employer's ceramics store, I had to swallow some strange jade beads so I could grab a white-hot whistle. Had the magic from the beads worn off yet?

"You are no regular werewolf," he whispered.

"Not even close." With my free hand, I scrambled to grab my goblin blade. The weapon lengthened as streaks of gold and black glowed on the hilt.

The shopkeeper eyed the sword and shied away. "You should be careful with that."

"I should say the same to you, pal."

He edged to the right, but I prepared to block my left. As expected, he feigned a shift to the right, but advanced from the other way. The man before me blurred, his shape twisting and unfurling. From between his golden feathers, I spied the lightning bird's obsidian claws and a red-chipped beak. His wings opened wide. The air crackled with static electricity. His beak swept forward, striking the blade with a loud *clang*. The blow shoved me into a home accent display, but I sidestepped in time and scrambled away.

"This isn't the place to fight." I gestured to all the *fragile* merchandise. "Can we take this outside?"

Umbane's wings fluttered in agitation. Another wave of heat hit my face. "I should eat before I work."

The term, *you're not yourself when you're hangry came to mind,* but I didn't say a word.

This time the lightning bird retreated, somehow stuffing himself through a human-sized open doorway. When he returned in human form again, he shook dust off his right shoulder.

"How about we start again?" I rested the tip of the goblin sword against the tile floor. The blade hadn't transformed back—which meant I had to keep my guard up. "Seamus sent me here to buy something from you. Can we make a deal?"

Umbane chuckled. "The leprechaun refuses to come to me."

"I wonder why. You tried to cook me broil-style."

He pursed his lips. "I don't eat people."

"Then did you want to drain my energy? Maybe skin me? If you planned to offer a two-for-one deal on one of those boob-looking lights, you've got horrible customer service skills."

"I would've drunk your blood and left you in the woods." He said this plainly as if we discussed the entrées at a fine eatery.

"I'm so *thankful?*"

"Yes, you should be." He missed the barb in my words. "You have the strength of a mountain. I like that."

Now that got a snort out of me.

The shop owner continued. "You are also more honorable than that nitwit leprechaun. He thought he could parade his women around me and I'd sell him another thunder feather."

"His methods are rather crass, but he must find you impressive. Even I thought your feathers were beautiful— and I've seen some gorgeous ones at the Gray Folk Feathers shop."

He grinned with pride. "I am Umbane, King of the Southern Shores. Guardian of the Hu'Dan Mountains." He went on for a bit with his honorific titles. "You are looking at the only Impundulu to grace these shores in a thousand years."

"Wonderful. How's business been the last thousand years?"

He frowned. "Not that good. Foot traffic went down when they diverted I-287. Even the supernaturals don't come here anymore since She Who Always Walks the Path is south of here. Sometimes I sell my feathers to pay my rent."

I folded my arms. "You said earlier you don't have any thunder feathers *yet*."

"A creature as magnificent as myself needs time to grow them."

"And how much time would that be?"

"About thirty days, maybe more."

Not good. "Do you mind if I call in two weeks to check your progress?"

"Why not pay a proper visit? Come for tea and conversation." He smiled, but all I saw was a chipped beak and claws. No thanks.

"'Cause I like having a pulse." I jerked my chin toward a stack of beautiful antique Christmas lamps. A SALE sign on top welcomed a wholesale purchase. We'd sold something similar at The Bends for a very nice price. "You have a large stock of those. Are you interested in selling any of them?"

"To Seamus?"

"Oh no, to a goblin retailer in South Toms River." I'd never bought stock for Bill before. His products simply showed up, but Bill never turned down a quick profit. Ever. The goblin could be on his deathbed and he'd negotiate coffin prices.

The lightning bird perked up and made an offer. We bounced back and forth—as one should do when dealing— and by the time we settled on a final price, I was as giddy as the days I shopped for myself. *And let's be honest, wouldn't my Christmas tree at home be even lovelier?*

Umbane hauled the boxed goods out to my Altima. "I hope to hear from you again—perhaps with some ideas on how I may modernize my store?"

"Sure."

If I got out of this alive, it wouldn't hurt for me to pass along a few pointers—like you shouldn't try to eat folks, especially the ones with cash to burn.

The lightning bird bid me farewell with a dip of his chin. As I pulled away, I said a prayer to every Russian saint I had on speed dial to get that man's feathers growing faster. Maybe I should have some growth lotion shipped his way, too. I laughed on my way home to South Toms River. My paws were empty and I had yet to buy anything for Seamus. The leprechaun wouldn't be pleased, while Bill would nod with approval.

"Profits before purchases," I could hear him say.

I couldn't see out of my rearview mirror, so it was best to drop these off at work before I headed home. Twenty minutes later, with smooth jazz music playing from my radio, I pulled into the parking lot at The Bends. This late at night, gloomy shadows draped the large, old building nestled between a parking lot and another flea market. Ramneil Pawn & Market had closed two weeks ago. Bill had yanked off the FOR SALE sign not long after it went up. He had plans to extend The Bends.

With two boxes tucked under each arm, I headed to the back dock, then through the set of double doors into the office. Hopefully Quinton, The Bends' janitor, could stuff these things into some corners. After that, I could catalogue them and put them up for sale during my next shift. The necromancer's telltale scent of frankincense and myrrh was faint—almost as if he hadn't been here recently.

"Quinton," I called out.

Humans did such a thing. They hoped saying a name would draw out that person from where they hid or worked elsewhere. But The Bends was deathly quiet—other than the creaks and yawns from wood stretching and contracting. I checked the rack where the necromancer hung his funeral march coat and found nothing there. A note on the Employee Safety board—a recent addition I added a couple years ago for the human inspectors—had a note from Quinton:

> *Bill,*
>
> *I'm heading off to my honeymoon. Not sure when I'll return. This is last minute, but my bride and I couldn't wait to elope.*
>
> *Sincerely,*
> *Quinton*

I chuckled a bit, glad to see he'd finally married his cemetery-roaming lady friend. The necromancer and I had gone on a date, and it hadn't gone well. Especially after one of his minions showed up in the waiter's uniform. Having Quinton off the market wouldn't be so bad.

Since our janitor was off enjoying some foggy bog off the beaten path, I stretched my back to haul in everything. Half of the red boxes weren't too sturdy, so I tossed those and grabbed some nice, empty brown ones from the back shelves. Gotta keep the kids safe these days. I left the first set of red and brown boxes near my computer and chair. When I turned around to get the next set, the seat rolled away from the merchandise.

Huh? That's new.

I approached the chair and gave it a push. Nothing. No sparks of magic, either. Matter of fact, the plastic appeared quite lifeless and boring. I shoved it back where it belonged, and this time the chair stayed put. Great.

Bill's place hid all sorts of secrets. When the basilisks attacked us, the building had kept everyone safe. After seeing all that, I shouldn't blink twice when a chair moved on its own. And yet, a question remained: *why* did it move?

I shuffled back, noting the chair hadn't moved. Good, time to get more done. I grabbed the rest of the boxes and arranged them in a neat pile. I could already imagine a lovely holiday display. The lights would glow with Christmas cheer and the warmth of my *babushka's* hugs. Bill wouldn't let me play holiday music this early in the year, but I might try. Especially if I can get folks in the mood to spend, spend, spend.

With everything done, I turned off the lights and escaped. While I closed the double doors, I ignored the sound of squeaky wheels as the chair rolled away from the boxes again.

CHAPTER THREE

The next morning, I got up long before the sun rose. A good night's sleep helped, but as a wolf of habit, I preferred to get up at a set time. My mate rolled over and pulled the covers over his face. Only tufts of his blond hair peeked out. Thorn Grantham could wake up if we had trouble, but if no one bothered him, he'd sleep until he had to get up for his shift as a manager up at the local mill.

The very idea of not getting up on time and just lying there drove me bonkers. Wasn't there always something to do? I hurried through my morning routine, slipping into jeans for dirty work instead of my standard pencil skirt and heels, and I got a carafe of coffee going. I even had food stowed away in plastic containers. My mom had been by, and she'd snuck food into the fridge.

"I don't know why you two don't come eat dinner every night," my mother complained. "He's too busy—you're too busy. It's *ploxha*. Bad. So I left you food. Warm it up and pretend you made it."

Thorn ate the food knowing damn well I hadn't made it.

I grabbed two dessert *piroshkis* from the fridge and put

them in the toaster oven to warm up. Once they were nice and toasty, I added a slab of butter and it melted off the side. *Perfection*, I thought with a sigh.

I stole a glance at my boxes of Christmas ornaments, holiday doodads, and wreaths lined up in the living room. My hoarded stash winked back at me. "Not as perfect as you guys," I added out loud.

With my mood lighter and my belly full of fluffy dough and spiced apples, I grabbed my purse and set out. I wanted to get to The Bend of the River Flea Market before two individuals dug into my boxes. I pulled up at work at least an hour before the store opened. Most days, I showed up right on time or at least ten minutes before the customers so I could check the floor for issues.

When I strode through the double doors to the dock, I held my breath and added steel to my spine. Walking in as an alpha female to the pack was one thing, but handling the two men sniffing their way around the boxes was another matter.

While I was out dealing with the demons at the ceramic shop, Bill had the genius idea to accept interns to give back to the goblin community. By the way, I'd used air quotes around the term, "give back." Profits always came first.

"What are you doing?" Every day I'd said hello, like any good Russian girl, but less than a week had left me like this.

"Where did these come from?" the first man named Wilhelm said.

Like the other intern, he had a slim build and wore wire-framed glasses. Wilhelm and August dressed in the standard startup business casual attire now, but when they'd first showed up, they didn't look that way. Back then, you'd think Bill had cloned himself. until he snapped, "You boys need to be distinguishable to the staff. I know I look handsome and all, but seeing my face every day is giving me the creeps, guys."

To appease their mentor, Wilhelm showed up with curly brown hair, like that painter Bob Ross, and August donned Hawaiian shirts. To most folks, they looked like brothers from the same family, but to my nose, it was as if the same person, namely Bill, had duplicated himself. It was weird as hell. (And I'm a werewolf.)

The temptation to peek under their glamour hit hard a couple of hours into working with them, but after they started following me around, I didn't care.

"Wilhelm said Bill forgot to invoice these," August said.

"Bill didn't forget anything," I said. "I'm the one who bought them."

Wilhelm's nose wrinkled up.

"When did these arrive?" August asked. Today, his bright yellow Hawaiian top had hallucination-inducing waves across the back and front.

"I bought them last night from a wholesaler up in Midland Park."

"What's the price point?" Wilhelm eagerly got too close. He even held—God help me—a copy of Bill's book: *Bill's Introduction to Management and Leadership.*

August rested his hand on his chin in a deep and thoughtful tech-CEO-manner. "If you bought them at fifteen dollars per unit, we could mark them up for three times the profit based on the demographics in the area."

"We were told we need a twenty-five thousand-dollar profit by the end of the quarter," Wilhelm added. "We should go as high as possible, then reduce the price to entice a sale."

Whenever they did these projections, I used to jump into the conversation with glee. Hell, I could go on for days comparing and contrasting the value of Victorian Christmas ornaments. But we all have our limits—and mine included discussing in-depth business projections about *everything* in the store.

To avoid them, I abandoned the conversation to sweep over the place before it opened. This pre-flight check used to take me five to ten minutes. With just one glance at the main store floor, I knew I'd need more time. At the registers on the far end of the room, I spotted the tip jars. We'd never used them before, just the usual little cups with a "Take a penny, leave a penny" signs. At the end of the workday, my boss always snatched up the coins, but at least we had them. Bill's little minions had left a generous-sized glass jar with the words TIP on top. To keep folks from giving coins, they'd added a dollar bill receptor to the side. After I'd almost smashed that thing into bits, I could see they'd put it back with a credit card reader, too.

Do you feel as slimy as I do right now?

Bill's greed had multiplied by two.

I grabbed a cardboard box from behind the counter, then unplugged the tip jar credit card reader. "Did you make sure this worked before you swindled the elderly and unsuspecting customers?"

Yep, they'd hooked up one of the broken units.

"It was stowed away with the rest of the readers." Wilhelm leaned toward August, and they had one of their many conversations in German and English. "Should we go check all of them?"

"God, no." As much as I'd like for them to service our tech, I couldn't help but imagine them hooking up a credit card reader to the public restroom.

Five bucks for a wee, the sign would read.

With the tip jar stowed away behind the counter, I hurried around to restock the glass displays with wands and hang mystical merchandise on the racks. I'd hoped—what a fool I am—after a day of observation, the pair would take over this task, but no, they returned to the back office to find something else to do.

Fifteen minutes later, The Bend of the River Flea Market opened, and summer shoppers spilled inside. This time we got lucky with a farmer's market down the road. The ladies in their straw hats and the gentlemen smelling of local wineries browsed our aisles with cash in their pockets. I left the main floor to the fire witch at the register and my assistant manager. She appeared in the nick of time.

Erica Holden strode into the store with a coffee in hand, her white sneakers barely blemished and her makeup light and tasteful. Her blonde hair was swept up into a ponytail, but it swung perfectly as she walked, almost as if a wind machine graced her presence with each step.

"Has our comedic duo rubbed your fur the wrong way yet?" She took a sip of her Americano. Damn, that coffee smelled good.

"They haven't stopped since yesterday," I whispered.

Erica and I had known each other for a long time. We had many issues before I became the alpha female of the pack, but this year we've gotten closer to that "meet in the middle" most folks liked.

I caught the sound of a box cutter from the back office. Those little meddlesome goblins...

"Go get 'em, I got the main floor," she said without blinking.

I returned to the back office to find them opening the first box. I forced myself to take a deep breath before I spoke. "Did Bill ask you to do that?"

"No, Mrs. Grantham," they both said at the same time.

"I'd like to add them into the system before we scatter the contents all over." Guess who'd have to clean that up, too? "Why don't you work on cleaning up the store next door?"

"Already done," August said proudly.

"Took us all weekend," Wilhelm added.

"There's still a hole—" August said.

"And other structural issues."

"Have you documented those?" I asked. The paper trail distraction worked seventy percent of the time.

"Of course," August said. "We had to finish that before Bill fixes up the place."

Didn't hurt to try.

I pushed my seat, which had somehow rolled all the way to the other side of the room, up to the workstation.

"What do you think the price should be, Mrs. Grantham?" August asked.

After typing in my password, I brought up the catalog system. "Don't know."

I did know, by the way. But I wasn't gonna go screaming down that black hole with them.

For ten minutes, I added a new item into the inventory management system with the interns staring over my shoulder. By the time I finished, I turned around to see them waiting.

"Don't you have something to do?" I asked. "A field to clear? I can get you another business textbook." I'd drive across the state to a specialty bookstore if necessary.

"Bill told us to listen and learn whenever you're around," Wilhelm said with pride.

My smile died. They took the word "listen" too far.

An idea came to mind. "How about you draft an ad for a new janitor? With Quinton out for a while, we'll need someone."

August grinned while Wilhelm turned to his companion with a burst of German.

"I must see the ad first." I gave them a stern eye like an adult would do to a pup. "And I'll be the one to submit it to the local paper." There was no way in hell I'd let them waltz into the *Toms River Gazette* with a train wreck of an announcement.

While The Bends intern team discussed how they'd look up, as they called it, an optimal job description, I escaped to the work floor. If those two spent all day figuring out a janitor's duties, my feelings wouldn't be hurt.

The day stretched out and my morning turned to the late afternoon. Aggie sent me a text message: *Can you pick me up tonight? My car won't start.*

At least she knew I'd be here late. The extended sale hours Bill added to help pay for the new property left me clicking the keys on the register and smiling until the clock hit nine in the evening. I could barely crack a grin as I turned off the workstation and high-tailed it to my car.

Those two probably had a magnum opus of all janitorial job descriptions, but I hadn't heard a peep out of them. Good. I stole a glance to the north where Sourland Natural Preserve lay. I welcomed any victory today.

My journey to Barney's restaurant took me to an eatery not far from the outskirts of town. Most of the werewolves ate at Archie's Burgers, but I liked how tidy Aggie kept the place as the manager. She'd also hired Brenna, an earth witch who I'd come to know as a good friend.

Since I'd missed the evening dining hours, Aggie, Brenna, and the other workers were cleaning up. They scrubbed down the blue painted tables and placed the black chairs on top.

My stomach growled in protest. I wished some sandwiches hid under the lemony fresh scent of bacteria-killing chemicals.

"Do you have anything to eat?" I asked.

"Everything's put away," Brenna said. "Want some chips?"

I shrugged. Chips were better than nothing.

The dark-haired witch fetched me a bag of Lay's. I fished in my purse for money, but she refused it.

"Thanks," I said.

"You look horrible," Aggie said as she counted the money at the register. My best friend from childhood never held back a punch.

"Your *pep* talks improve every time we chat." The bag opened with a pop and I tossed down one.

"Nobody seems to want to hear the truth from her," Brenna said, flashing me her dimpled grin.

"Wow, do I look that bad?" I glanced at my jeans, horrified to find them dusty and my shirt had dirt on the side. "I must be really tired."

"Or maybe you've had *personal* growth," Aggie chimed in after freeing her red hair from a bun.

"Something is growing on me, and it isn't my sense of self-care." I turned to Brenna. "Do you need a ride, too? I don't see your car out front."

"No need. My mom is coming." Brenna switched out of her work shoes for some comfortable loafers. "She wanted to have the 'talk' about me not returning to Europe to teach."

Brenna told me she used to teach at a prestigious medical school. She jumped over the pond because of Nick, my white wizard friend, which I found pretty cool. Nick deserved to have someone willing to dig into his trench-coat-covered veneer to find the awesome guy underneath.

"Honestly, I'm used to those conversations. My family tends to meddle."

Aggie belted out a laugh as she turned off the lights in the seating area. "Meddle? Is that what you call it?"

I cringed, knowing what she meant.

"They mean well," I admitted.

Aggie pursed her lips and glanced at Brenna. "This name tag would've said Aggie Stravinsky—"

"Oh, stop it." I tried to hide a giggle and failed.

Aggie ushered us out the door, mimicking one of my aunts with ease. "You don't need just *any* man. You're Irish right? Well, that means you need a good, strong man. A *Russian* man."

Thank goodness Brenna's mom was waiting outside the door in a VW van. The elder earth witch called out the window. "Hey, girls!"

Brenna waved and jumped into the car.

I thought I'd opened myself to more teasing from Aggie, but the moment we got into the car, she pulled out her phone to type a text. The temptation to ask how she was doing hit me hard. We hadn't chatted since I'd stopped working for the demons. Was she seeing anyone new? Had she heard anything from her estranged father, that kind of thing. Over the years, we'd drifted apart now and then, but when we reunited it was as if no time had passed at all.

I dropped her off and headed home. The night's chorus of frogs and crickets floated through my open window, and I smiled at the nearly full moon.

"Hey, pretty girl," I whispered.

The glow illuminated my dashboard and ushered me home. The full moon had passed a couple days ago, but I couldn't wait to shed this human skin again. Every trivial thing the human agonized over disappeared.

Soon enough, I arrived home down the long winding path to the cottage I shared with Thorn. I was surprised to see Rex's truck next to Thorn's SUV. My husband's best friend had avoided me lately. He had yet to cure his asshole disease, but the more we kept apart, the better.

I went inside, finding the house quiet, but voices floated over from the backyard. Was something wrong with Thorn? Too curious for my own good, I made a beeline for the bathroom bordering the back of the house. After turning on the sink, I listened to their conversation.

"You can't keep taking care of them," Thorn said, his voice quieter.

"It's not that simple," Rex replied.

"Yes, it is. If people don't want to do better, your efforts won't make them care."

I ran my hands through the cool water, knowing who they were talking about. Thorn had revealed not too long ago how Rex's brothers had fallen into a bad spot and he was now supporting them financially.

"I'm tired of giving a shit," Rex admitted. "So damn tired."

With those words, I turned off the water. Shame circled my chest as I abandoned the bathroom. As much as I didn't like Rex, nobody should have to shoulder the burden of irresponsible people. Even if they were your family.

CHAPTER FOUR

June jumped out of the window and July swept in. Standing in the relentless Manhattan heat didn't help. I about panted as I fanned my shirt to circulate cool air down my chest.

At least I had something to do instead of dwelling on my problems. Briefly, the weight of Diana's collar circled my throat. I gasped and bit out a curse. I hadn't told Thorn or anyone else about my fears. How I was scared as hell I'd end up captured again. A couple of days ago, I drove Aggie home and that would've been the perfect time to say something. Hell, we could've talked about the weather, but I'd dug the deepest hole in my soul and buried the danger.

I didn't want the people I loved to face the inevitable with me.

To get back on track, I focused on the task at hand. I stood only ten feet from my next assignment at West 4th and Mercer Street.

Back at the leprechaun's place, he'd left me an envelope with a shiny pearl and a note:

> Head on uptown to My Sweet Baby Monster.
> I need you to buy a rare silver baby rattle.
> One of my ladies will drop off something to
> barter. That rattle will fetch a nice price for a
> private seller.

I eyed the ten-floor pre-war building and my eyes formed slits. If Seamus or one of his ladies couldn't march in there and snag it, something had to be up.

A quick search online revealed this building only had residential units. The top floor, where the shop should've sat, only had a penthouse unit drenched in black. Lovely.

To be careful, I circled the block and walked down the alley. Might as well try the old-fashioned way and see if I could walk in. Shouldn't be hard, right?

I squinted at the top floor and pried at the magic hiding what I sought. Seconds passed as I clawed and clawed at it until flecks of crystalline light glinted through the chaotic cover. Less than a minute later, a tenth-floor storefront with a neon sign appeared. Garish pink and blue lights circled the store name.

Gotcha, you sneaky bugger.

I strode through the glass door into a lobby with shiny tiled floors. Not a single box had a last name. Matter of fact, all the slots for names were empty. Which could mean nothing these days because of privacy concerns, but my hackles were already raised. Everything felt too normal. Too human.

After I hurried over to the elevator, I pushed the UP button. I waited for the familiar ding but none came. I stabbed the button again. Finally, the door slid open to a crack. A fog of cinnamon drifted out while murky, grayish-green darkness circled within.

Nope. Don't you dare try to open it, my paws warned me.

I pressed the button again. Much harder.

A ribbon of black smoke seeped out of the opening and nipped at my hand. I jumped back with a growl. Damn it. Why hadn't I brought the goblin blade?

After I beat a hasty retreat down the street to a quaint little deli, I considered my options. I could scale the building —not from the front, of course—but from the back came to mind. Back in Russia, I'd done such a thing to save Thorn, but now I had *a lot* less bravado. Only a fool marched into a spellcaster's domain. Therefore, I had to consider other possibilities. Time to call in reinforcements.

A call to Brenna's phone went through quickly.

"Hey Nat, what's up?" she asked.

"Not sure how to broach this, but I could use a hand."

That got me a laugh in return. "What trouble are you in now?" Brenna purred.

I rolled my eyes.

Another familiar voice bled through the line, along with the roar of a TV commercial. "Is that Nat?" Aggie asked. "Tell her to come over and bring snacks. She *hates* this show, but she can pretend she likes it to humor us."

"I am in a bit of a bind," I said. "I need to get into a building locked with magic. There's a bunch of sigils above the elevator. Can I send you some photos?"

"Sure, send them my way."

I shot the photos over to Brenna while she stayed on the line. Meanwhile, the waitress at the deli brought me over a cup of hazelnut coffee and a generous piece of strawberry cheesecake. "What're you two doing?" I asked.

"We're watching that hoarder show. You know, the one where a crew helps people clean out their houses?"

"Uh, huh." I took a huge bite of cheesecake to swallow down what I really thought about the show. I'd come to terms with the fact I was a hoarder, but I didn't need a reminder. Might as well slap a mirror in front of the TV, I say.

"Whoa, this is bad," Brenna said. "Where are you?"

"Manhattan. I'm buying a rattle for that leprechaun. Is there any way to get past those sigils and get to the top floor without climbing up the side?"

"Not without a spellcaster. That whole building is enchanted. Those sigils are supposed to protect you from what's inside." She snorted. "Only powerful witches can create these. Most people don't go to places like this, but Nick told me you're *not* most people. I say you shouldn't go there if you value your life."

My white wizard friend had told her *way* too much. "I gotta get in. Is there any way you can help? And I'll owe you one, if you can."

"Are you in trouble again?" Aggie griped. She'd heard every word.

"It's not that bad, Aggie," I said.

"Yeah right," she replied.

I caught the sounds of rustling. Someone turned off the TV. What were they doing?

Brenna sighed over the line. "Aggie, we are not taking the pizza with us."

"The hell we're not," Aggie retorted. "I got half off for the pineapple pizza Friday deal."

Another exasperated breath from Brenna. "We're on our way. I know *exactly* where you are so don't go in there. I mean it."

Less than a half hour later, I finished my food and Brenna showed up with Aggie. As expected, my best friend showed up ready to kick some ass in leather pants and boots. She'd tried to tame her red hair in a bun, but a bunch of curly strands had made a run for it. Brenna wore a jean jacket, jeans, and heels. Her short bob was slicked back.

"What do we need to get for that sleazy dirtbag again?" Aggie asked.

I explained everything as Brenna sized up the building.

"So all he wants is some silver rattle?" Aggie asked.

"Yeah, and I just can't pick up one of those from Costco. Is there any way to get past the wards?" I asked Brenna.

"The only way to find out is to try to get in." The witch sauntered through the door, and her heels clicked on the marble floor. With each step, the floor reverberated with a strange energy. The hum creeped up my legs and settled into my belly.

We reached the elevator in question. The door was shut this time.

Brenna pressed the button.

"This is when things went crazy," I said.

When the elevator doors opened, I steeled myself for a fight, but all we found was a simple elevator with garish green paint and bright lights shining from above.

"No monsters here," Aggie said. "Yet."

"This whole place has a bump-in-the-night vibe." I was the last one to get on, while Aggie had sashayed her way inside.

As to be expected, the elevator had ten buttons, but the golden tiles surrounded the knob for the tenth floor with more sigils. I reached over to press the tenth-floor button, but Brenna snatched my wrist.

"It's cursed." She plucked out her oak wand from within her jean jacket. Using the end, she poked the button. So even the witch couldn't touch it.

I stared a bit at the panel to see if I could pry apart the magic, but nothing budged—which was never a good sign.

The ride up to the tenth was a silent one where no one spoke and only the sound of the crank and whirl of the elevator heading upward filled the space. When the doors opened, a shiny store with pleasant music appeared.

Compared to many of the mom-and-pop supernatural stores I've seen, this one had the gleam and glitz of an upper-crusty boutique. We passed dust-free mahogany shelves and state of the art TVs advertising goods. A lovely display with what had to be a horse's harness had a spotlight shining on it from above. On the other side of the store, next to the glass counters, sat rows of steel cages.

Aggie's gaze swept over the store. "What is this shit?"

My thoughts exactly.

Based on the name My Sweet Baby Monster, and what I needed to buy, this place had to be some type of baby shop. But what kind of baby shop had harnesses, collars, and other restraints?

I made my way toward what had to be the main counters with the registers, but no one was around. Not a single scent or sound either, other than the pleasant Baby Shark music playing. Cheerful cartoons played on the television attached to the far end of the room. The TV was on mute, but the show's bubbly animated characters stood out compared to the elaborate leashes and chains in leopard prints and pastel colors.

"When you and Thorn decide to pop out a couple of pups, you should get one of these cute little cribs with a cage on top," Aggie said with a wink.

"Sure." There was no way in hell I was adding My Sweet Baby Monster into any future baby shower registry.

I searched for the rattle, unable to find it among the items in the first or second aisle.

"Why don't we split up so we can find it faster?" I suggested.

"No one is walking alone in here," Brenna said firmly.

"Seems harmless." Aggie flicked a baby mobile with creepy plastic skulls. "Where's the staff?"

"That's why I don't want us splitting up," Brenna said. "My mom warned me about places like this one. Regular witches don't go here. They send minions if they need this kind of stuff. Not that I'd buy this weird crap," she added when we gave her a strange look.

"Speaking of relationships," I said to lighten the mood, "How are things going with Nick?"

"Things are fine. We don't speak as much since he's been pretty busy this semester over in medical school. I'd like to see him when he's on break in August, but I don't know if I'm heading over to Europe or if he's coming here."

I finally spotted a set of silver rattles sitting on a red velvet tray in a glass display against the wall.

"Are things serious?" Aggie's grin widened. "I've seen the way he looks at you. I think he's serious. Are you feeling the same way, too?"

Brenna flashed a pensive face as I examined the pieces. "I think so. We've been through some major stuff the last couple of months and I still like him. He's met my parents, and other than his little collecting habit, I could see us settling down someday."

I grinned. "So what does it mean when witches and wizards settle down?" I asked. Over the years, I'd wondered about this. Did witches and wizards have regular families like humans? Did they have mortgages? Maybe they grumbled about who made dinner materialize on the table or who made time for their kids' Little League games? It was hard to believe they had regular ole lives like everyone else.

Brenna stopped in the middle of the aisle. The witch's heartbeat shot through the roof as Aggie bumped into her.

"What's up?" Aggie touched Brenna's shoulder.

"Both of you shouldn't move," Brenna breathed.

"Where are they?" I froze. My gaze swept over the store. Nothing moved except for a swiveling TV. Then I caught it—the faint shifting of cloth brushing against the floor—not from someone's clothing.

From around a pillar, a short, bronzed-skinned woman appeared wearing a nun's habit. She clasped her hands together and rested them on her flat stomach. The woman peered at us with interest and looked like any other Catholic nun—except for the fact she didn't have any fingernails or eyebrows.

My mouth dropped open. I croaked, "Good evening, do you work here?"

Brenna's head slowly turned to me and the look she flashed me definitely said I-told-you-not-to-move.

"You need to do a better job restraining your animals," the woman said pleasantly. "I'm Sister Reyes. How can I help you?"

"These wolves are under my protection." Brenna respectfully inclined her head. "I'm here as a patron. And they're not my *animals*."

"You're not here to shop," the nun said crisply. "The dark-haired wolf wants something." Her head turned far too quickly. "The other one smells like trouble."

Aggie's straight face stretched into a feline grin.

I gave Brenna a reassuring nod and introduced myself. "I'm here to barter for a silver rattle."

The nun took one step forward. Suddenly, she stood before me.

A menacing growl seeped out of Aggie. I froze as Brenna murmured, "Don't move this time."

Now that the nun loomed close enough to smack me, I caught a whiff of vanilla perfume. The vanilla masked something like vinegar. The sour, musty scent grew stronger as if something large crept into the store.

I glanced upward. Blinked twice to break through the magic. Sister Reyes's appearance changed before me as if I flipped between channels.

"These definitely aren't your animals." Her human mouth widened into a smile that briefly flashed in my mind to an elongated tongue over serrated teeth. "This one still bears the stench from a divine collar."

My stomach dropped ten floors. How did she know?

"Excuse me?" Brenna murmured.

"Her life is a vine with many paths snipped and re-grafted in place to save her life, but the end is near." Sister Reyes' head tilted in sympathy. "Her enemies are gathering. Their claws are scratching the dirt in anticipation, their mouths gnawing at their chains to come find her."

She turned to me. "And you will not survive when you meet them."

Aggie pulled me back. "Apparently, common sense isn't for sale here. Fuck this shit."

It took me a moment to remember why I was here. "Thanks for the *advice,* but I need to buy that silver rattle." The confidence in my voice had beaten a hasty retreat out. "I have a beautiful blue pearl to barter, if you'd like."

The nun frowned and the sourness flared. "That degenerate sent you here, didn't he?"

She advanced forward. Grew two inches. "You used the witch to get in here. Then you threaten me by drawing that heathen to my doorstep—"

Brenna stepped in front of me. Her oak wand vibrated in her hand. "Stand down!"

The creature hiding behind the nun's façade revealed herself. With clawed fingers extended, she came at us.

Brenna raised her wand high as bright light engulfed the store. I had to shut my eyes.

"Oh, shit!" Aggie yanked again to signal our retreat, but I didn't budge.

The nun scampered backward and I opened my eyes to find her not against the back wall, but hanging from the ceiling.

"What are you doing?" Aggie barked at me. "Is the rattle worth your life?"

"And what if Diana is coming for me?" I shouted at the nun. "Give me the rattle for the pearl and I'll go. No harm. No foul."

"Whatever you're doing, you need to do it quickly," Brenna whispered. "I can't use that spell again. That manananggal is too powerful."

I took a step forward. "You want me out, so barter with me and our business will be done."

The manananggal's teeth clicked loud enough to bite my ears. "Take it and go." With a flick of her filthy fingers, the glass display's lock opened. I hurried over to the display and left the pearl on the velvet tray in the rattle's place.

My friends and I hightailed it out of there. By the time we reached the street, the sour feeling in my stomach eased.

I'd done it, but the hard look on Aggie's face stopped me cold.

"You have some explaining to do," she said far too quietly.

CHAPTER FIVE

I'd like to say the conversation on the way home sounded like, "Gee, it must be scary having hellhounds and a vengeful goddess coming for you," but that didn't happen. Matter of fact, I was burned from the proverbial flames coming off Aggie's body. As I drove the others home, Brenna kept trying to chat with Aggie, but my best friend reflected a stony silence. Not once did she look at me either. Most of the time, she had *plenty* to say, but for once she ignored me—which hurt more than her usual verbal thrashings.

Once we arrived at Aggie's apartment complex, she left with a curt, "Bye."

Brenna said, "Wow, she's super pissed about Diana."

"No, she isn't mad," I replied. "Aggie only speaks to stand up for me. She can't save me this time."

"I thought once Mevelyn took your place you were free from the huntress?"

Briefly, sorrow circled my chest. Karey's aunt had taken my place and now she lived as Diana's prisoner. I pulled away from Aggie's apartment and tried to focus on driving. "Mevelyn simply bought me more time."

~

The next morning, I didn't wake up chipper and ready to sell flea market goods.

As I drove to The Bends with the smooth sounds of Nat King Cole blasting out of my Nissan's speakers, I considered what it meant to have more time. Over the past couple of years, I'd worked my ass off for *more* of anything. More time to fix my relationship with my family. More time to reunite with Thorn, the love of my life.

I hit the parking lot at The Bends. Sure enough, the Saturday morning diehards already waited under the awnings for their flea market fix. One brownie, four fire witches, and Mrs. Kite, the harpy, formed a lopsided line. When that bird-like creature caught sight of me, she grinned. And not in a good way. Guess Mrs. Kite wanted another refund.

With the customers' eyes boring a hole through my back, I hurried to the far end of the store, passing our awning-covered tables. Waves of heat baked the top of my head. I dreaded coming back out. I strolled toward the store and stopped cold. There were a couple of roof shingles sprinkled across the back dock. After a quick glance upward, I spied the missing sections. Were those two goblin apprentices up to no good again? They were probably following Bill's orders to remove the charitable bins near the registers. But then again, the store always seemed to maintain itself.

The back door opened. Rex walked out wearing a work apron. He bent over and stuffed the shingles into a cardboard box. When he spotted me approaching, his face bunched up with distaste.

"What are you doing here?" I knew very well why he was here, but I had to ask.

"Not sure what happened up there, but these keep falling down."

Another shingle rained down and Rex sidestepped it. Both our gazes shot upward. I spied another piece teetering on the edge. Underneath the spot where it had lain, a strange sheen glimmered with a mossy green color. Almost like flecks of emerald.

"I need to put up a sign or grab a ladder and get up there," he said with a frown. "Someone could get hurt."

I got to the point first. "Who hired you?"

"One of those two fellows inside. Wasn't sure which one, but some guy named August called me up and gave me an interview over the phone." He shrugged before he added, "He hired me right then and there."

I bit my lower lip. The need to say something not so *nice* came to mind, but I kept my mouth shut. Of course, those two damn apprentices hired Rex without so much as checking his background. Or whether that man fought with authority figures at any opportunity.

I marched into The Bends and found Wilhelm sitting behind Bill's desk. For some reason, he was ordering more merchandise from yet another overseas wholesaler.

"What are you doing?" I asked.

"Bill told me to order more stock from Germany," he declared proudly. "Can't wait to see the profits."

"I mean who signed off on hiring Rex without my input?" I asked.

"Mr. Chapman's been working since 3 a.m." While Wilhelm spoke, his glamour flickered in and out. The goblin's skin flashed green, then a warm peach color spilled into his skin again. "He's not as fast as he said he was on the phone, but he should make do while Quinton's gone."

Did he really just ignore my question? Yep.

"Is there something wrong with your...masking spell? You're looking a bit greenish."

"Something is wrong on the sales floor," he explained. "I think the humans can see through my magic."

I mentioned the roof problem. "Something is up. I don't think it's you. I think it's the store."

The wolf within me rattled at its cage, suddenly alarmed. I left the back room to scan the sales floor to see if anything else had gone awry. The last thing we needed was the fire witch burning the place down, or one of the human clerks losing their damn minds.

A quick sweep over the sales floor revealed nothing until I glanced up. The flea market's rafters had always been free from cobwebs and dust. They were clean thanks to my hard work, but the last time I'd scaled up there I hadn't seen the cracks in the wood paneling.

I strolled through The Bends until I caught a gasp from a customer. I rushed over to see the glass display, which was filled with wands, spitting out its contents onto the floor. An elderly man in a baseball jersey and shorts scrambled back as he was pelted with wooden sticks.

"Oh dear," I said, flashing an apologetic smile. I scrambled to snatch up the wayward wands. One nearly took my eye out. "Looks like someone overpacked these."

The man grimaced and hurried after his companion. "Did you see those things just fly out?"

"Oh, c'mon, Stanley," the woman replied.

By the time I got the merchandise back into the case, the staff had wrangled up cast off magical capes and swept up billowing medieval bloomers. The poor human clerks appeared confused, and the fire witch was wide-eyed.

"Have you seen Bill this morning?" I asked Millicent.

The fire witch shook her head while she grabbed a pack

of cigarettes from her pocket. "You're the first manager I've seen on the floor. I dunno what's going on, but the magic in this place is all wonky."

"Do you know what's up?"

"Not a clue." Her hands trembled as she edged closer to the door. "Best I can do is blow stuff up, to be honest."

"You go take that break." *At a safe distance from the building* was my next thought.

I returned to the back office wishing I could join the fire witch for a de-stress session with some smokes. Wilhelm had vanished. Lovely. I checked for August or even Bill, but spotted not a single goblin. As the only manager, I shouldn't leave to search for them, but these problems were outside of my pay grade. After circling the desks twice, I caught a goblin scent—an earthy one with the heavy tang of iron. Whether it belonged to Bill, Wilhelm, or even August, I wasn't sure. Goblins did a great job of masking themselves. The trail led me out of The Bends and past the docks. More shingles littered the area and I avoided those. For now, anyway.

The July humidity hit the moment I strode across the field between The Bends' lot and the empty store next door. The new site needed work. The last owner, a jovial lady who wore way too many rings and had a massive collection of muumuus, had let the siding go moldy and the white paint chipped off. Over the years, I assumed she'd rebuild and get the place up to code. She ended up losing the place and been foreclosed on. Now weeds and stacks of abandoned building supplies reigned in the back.

A quick circle around the building got me nowhere so I unlocked one of the side entrances. The scent grew stronger, along with something else. The smoky undertone scorched the back of my throat as I crept past glass displays covered in filthy gray tarps. I would've expected Bill, as money-hungry as he was, to have already re-purposed the retail fixtures.

Even if Bill was dying on his deathbed, he wouldn't have left this place to fester.

Carefully, I ventured farther inside until I found the source of the smell. Lying prone near the metal stands, August stared back at me, wide-eyed and very much dead.

CHAPTER SIX

"Bill, pick up the phone." My third call jumped straight to voicemail.

Every time I pressed the call button, I expected to hear Bill's grumbly voice. The clinks from the cash he counted would filter through the connection and I could pretend all was right with the world. Bill would calmly show up and take over. With a snap of his fingers, things would go back to normal.

The frantic chaos at The Bends continued around me while I hid in the comparatively tranquil back office. The fire witch continued to chain smoke on the back dock, and Rex had already filled another box with roof shingles.

Having seen his friend's body, a wide-eyed Wilhelm stumbled across from the other lot, then sat forlorn in one of the seats. His glamour flickered in and out, revealing his green slumped shoulders and misshapen head.

I gave up calling for a moment. "When was the last time you saw August?" I asked.

"This morning. He said something about cleaning the floor. August thought Rex didn't do a good job."

"So Rex was here early with August, then everyone else showed up for their shift?"

"Yeah, if anyone else had snooped around here, I would've seen them, but then again, we get deliveries overnight, so anyone could've been in and out."

Years ago, I'd set up cameras in the back office to maintain quality controls. But we never added any cameras on the back dock or even toward the other lot. We'd never had any break-ins or any crimes. A couple of the local kids had tried to spray graffiti on the side of the building, but The Bends' wards usually cleaned them off by the time the store opened.

"Did Bill tell you about a trip or anything?" I asked.

"He hadn't mentioned anything, but I know he's likely searching for what's wrong with The Bends."

At least Bill was trying to fix *something*. I shot off another text message. This one had a bit of a bite. Bill still didn't respond.

I stalked the path between the desks. "Can you call Bill or maybe send him a text message? None of my calls are going through."

The goblin picked up his cell, an ancient flip phone, and typed out a message. Less than a minute later, the phone vibrated with a response.

Wilhelm glanced up at me. "He's on his way."

"How did you get through to him? Does he have a private line I don't know about?"

"I sent the message in Old German. I added that the place was on fire, *and* we had a bomb threat." He had a straight face while he said this.

I nodded. He did what he had to do, and we needed help now. Not later. Something was going down. Was Bill under attack? Had an old enemy of his made an appearance? I knew all too well what it was like to have folks pop up seemingly out of nowhere to exact revenge. Those adversaries were the most dangerous. You never saw them coming.

A couple minutes later, Bill appeared. Like Wilhelm, his glamour never snapped in place, but he looked better than his apprentice. As my goblin boss walked up to me, his demeanor defiant and determined, another idea stabbed the back of my mind: maybe this enemy wasn't Bill's, but mine.

"It's a mess here," I whispered.

"No shit," he said gruffly. "The shop is one wiggly worm right now. Can't seem to get a good grip on it."

"What about August?" I asked softly.

"I've taken care of the body already. It's not out in the open for the police to come across it." Bill turned to Wilhelm. "Also, I don't like it when *people* make threats over secure lines," he added.

"I didn't know what to do." Wilhelm's head lowered. "I saw him not long after Mrs. Grantham found him. Something powerful had killed him—it had sucked out his essence and left him with nothing."

"Do you know what could've done that to him?" I placed my hands on my hips, considering every foe I'd faced. Many of them, including warlocks, could've killed August.

"Could be many things," Bill replied. "Many creatures have kicked me when I was down. Either August got in an intruder's way or someone targeted him. Who knew he'd be here this morning?"

"That's only you, me, Erica, and Wilhelm. Maybe Rex, too."

Bill pushed his glasses up. "I can't think of a reason why someone would kill him—unless they're the competition. I had a great sale last week."

I gave Bill a dark look hot enough to rival the heat outside. Sale or not, employees shouldn't *die* at work. "This might all have to do with the craziness here. The Bends has been poisoned by a spell or a curse of some kind."

Bill, Wilhelm, and I bounced ideas back-and-forth. We discussed the schedule for the last forty-eight hours. Who came and went, were there any changes in routine. That kind of thing.

"Is it possible August had an enemy and they showed up to kill him?" I asked.

"He doesn't seem like the type," Rex said as he came inside to dump another box in a corner. "When I saw him this morning, he appeared agitated and didn't say much. But the scent he gave off smelled fearful. Matter of fact, he wouldn't shut up about everything he wanted me to do."

"There must be something else. This whole place feels off," Bill said.

"What about those lamps Natalya brought in the other day?" Rex suggested. "Some of the crushed boxes from the lamps had a scent I've never smelled before."

"What weird smell?" When I'd picked up the lamps from the lightning bird, the stock smelled brand-spanking new.

"I'm not sure. It was like old beer. What I do know is the lamps *and* the boxes had that scent this morning," Rex explained.

"The lamps were in red boxes," I said. "I put some of them into brown ones. Which boxes smelled weird?"

"Both of them."

Well, that didn't narrow down the source.

"Damn it." Bill slowly shook his head. "Where did you get those things again?"

"I got them from a lightning bird north of here." I explained how I brought in the merchandise and replaced some of the broken boxes. So the problem either started here or jumped into our lap from somewhere else. Also, we'd sold a third of the lamps—which meant a lot of them were out in the wild now.

"Call the bird," Bill said firmly. "Find out what's going on."

I headed out to the docks to make the phone call. Rex trailed after me, his eyes hard on my back as he leaned against the wall. I'd ask for privacy, but then again werewolf hearing meant he'd hear everything either way. The phone rang five times before the lightning bird picked up.

We went through pleasantries before I got to the heart of the matter.

"That sounds horrible," Umbane said, "but I don't think there's anything wrong with the lamps."

"We're checking for anything peculiar," I replied. "Your shop might've been affected, too. Where did you get the lamps from?"

"I bought them from a yatsukahagi from Connecticut." He read off an address and shop name. "I got a pretty good deal, and my customers love variety."

I loved *variety* too, but not the chaotic kind. Something about the name of that shop sounded familiar. While the lightning bird shuffled through the papers on his desk to verify his purchase, I checked the latest message from that damn leprechaun.

Umbane repeated the same name in my text message.

> For your next task, I need you to pick up a silk shawl from my spider friend at the Arachne Attire Emporium in Fairfield, Connecticut. I've already paid, but the yatkuhsaghi hasn't followed through yet. Give them a nudge, as they say in the business. Go to 928 Fairfield...

Bill did not take the news of the connection well. "Just one damn problem after another."

While I finished chatting with the lightning bird, Bill

opened a hole in the floor using goblin magic. With a wave of his hands, the remaining lamps marched over and tossed themselves inside. The hole closed with a loud slurp. My heart broke to see Christmas careening into oblivion.

"I need to leave again," Bill said.

"What about the store? Do we need to close?"

"I can't manipulate or stop it. What I *can* do is go to the spider shop."

"Why do you want to go there?" I asked. "Maybe the lamps are just cursed."

The goblin frowned. "This isn't some everyday spell like those sad-looking capes on the store floor. The magic in those lamps is dangerous. Back in the Dark Ages, if you wanted to take out the competition's cart, you poisoned the horse. I'm wondering if that spider is behind all this."

"Have you ever been to that place before?" I explained how Seamus wanted me to go there and buy a silk garment from the shop.

Bill's brow furrowed and I briefly caught a flare of his anger. "Nope, but I'm going to see what they're up to. I don't know if Seamus is behind this or the spider or that lightning bird, but either way, you're heading up there today and I'm going with you." Bill shifted his attention to the apprentice. "You're coming with us too, kid. Can't have you frightening the customers."

CHAPTER SEVEN

After a deathly silent two-hour car ride up I-99 along the coastline, Bill, Wilhelm, and I reached the seaside town of Fairfield, Connecticut. Like any summer beach town, tourists flocked the small mom-and-pop cafes and shops to enjoy the 4th of July weekend. Banners draped on power line stands caught the wind as families walked down Fairfield Beach Road to the nearby beaches.

I rolled down the window to sample the pleasant breeze. With everything I had to do today, I'd miss out on the pack's annual barbecue up at Double Trouble State Park. The Daltons planned a huge pig roast and the Stravinskys always brought my favorite dishes. Guess I'd have to enjoy the leftovers again.

I still counted down the days until Thorn and I could take a proper vacation to Maine for a fishing trip. We could've even ended up in a place like this one, spending our hot summer days hanging out on a boat in the many reservoirs around here. I'd wear a sun hat and catch up on my reading while Thorn caught fish after fish.

Instead of pulling up next to a cozy cabin, we arrived in front of Arachne Attire Emporium. Time to get to work.

Wilhelm peered at me from the back seat. The remaining goblin apprentice hadn't said a thing during the ride. Before we'd left The Bends, he'd spoken to Bill in German. My German was far too rusty to understand what they had said, but I couldn't miss Bill's narrowed eyes or his pinched nose.

Bill got out of the car first and approached the front. The clothing shop, like the bookstore and aromatic seasoning shop next door, had dated wooden siding and overpainted windowsills. Through the bookstore's window, I noticed patrons milling about while the seasoning shop was empty.

I expected Bill to march right in, but he waited as if he sized up the place. Did he sense any danger? I glanced from the doorway to my employer.

We walked into the shop, and instead of bells on the door, a chime sounded with our arrival. The chime was connected to a long string strung from the glass door and disappeared into the murkiness in the back. Like any clothing store that had wares for humans, the front had racks with brightly colored silk shirts and blouses, along with maxi dresses and fitted pants.

After I took two steps inside, a lingering scent buried underneath the garments crossed my nose. The musky scent, almost like rotted mushrooms, smelled like a shallow grave.

An older Asian man stepped out of the blackness in the rear. He wore a green long-sleeved silk shirt and trousers. Tufts of white hair peeked out from under his baseball cap. When I smiled, he didn't return the gesture.

"What business do you have here?" the man asked Bill.

Apparently, there'd be no "how may I help you" or "is there anything that you'd like to try on?"

I stepped forward. "I'm a buyer for Seamus. Are you the manager?"

At the mention of Seamus's name, the elderly gentleman briefly bared his tiny, yellowed teeth.

"He told me I needed to fetch a silk shawl from you," I said softly. "He already sent the payment."

Bill folded his arms and tilted his head to the side. His gaze sharpened behind his wide framed glasses. For once, I wished I could see the magical world through Bill's eyes. He'd cast a spell over me to reveal some of the supernatural world's secrets, but I surmised he could see much more. So far, I'd yet to peek behind the silk shop owner's proverbial curtain of magic. Every supernatural place I'd encountered so far had hidden craziness, so I expected no different from this one.

"I happened to come across lamps that were bought wholesale from your shop," my boss said. "Those lamps have caused *problems*."

The tone was sharp enough to make the shopkeeper pull off his cap. He ran his clawed fingers over a bald spot on the top of his head. His mouth opened slightly, revealing a blackened tongue.

I bit my lower lip as firecrackers popped in the distance. Could Bill have at least waited until I got what I needed?

"Lamps?" the man said bitterly. "I don't know what you're talking about."

I hurried to add, "The other day I bought some holiday lamps from Umbane, the lightning bird. Do you know him?"

The older gentleman nodded. "I sold him those lamps about a month ago. At the time, the stock was clean. I always sell clean goods."

"Well, you were mistaken," Bill said. "Those things were tainted with magic, and you better tell me where you got them."

The silk shop owner edged toward us this time. Wilhelm took a step back. Bill refused to budge.

"Are you implying I sell tainted goods, Goblin?" He crushed his baseball cap in his clenched fist. "You can't simply come and go as you please making accusations without proof."

"If you're not guilty," Bill said with a twirl of his fingers, "then you should have no problem proving the goods you sell are clean. Somehow, your lamps or your boxes were tainted before they ended up in my place of business." The side of the goblin's mouth tilted up in a grin. "Do you have any proof?"

"I'm sure he does. Just let him explain," I bit out.

"Tread carefully, Goblin." The old man's voice sounded far deeper—far bigger than what his tiny frame could produce. "The last time I dealt with your people back in Yokohama, they never tried to cross me again."

More firecrackers sliced through the air, but they seemed to hit different with the strange hum in the store.

"I highly doubt you've faced any goblin and walked away," Bill replied. "Your threats are empty, Spider."

"We shall see." The older man became a blur, and he lashed out. At first, I glimpsed something dark and furry coming at me. No, not me. A nimble spider's legs and body shot out of the man's belly and grasped Wilhelm by the side. The goblin apprentice squeaked as a human-sized arachnid's fangs bit into his shoulder. The poor goblin's arm flopped off and hit the floor with a thud.

I growled and reached for the goblin blade on my ankle. I didn't forget it this time.

My goblin employer stepped in front of me. Breathtaking magic with the scent of red pepper flared from him. With an upward flick of his pale fingers, the floorboards swung upward, tossing up Wilhelm and the spider. They slammed into the ceiling, then tumbled into a clothing rack. Dust rained down on us.

I pulled out the glimmering goblin blade, hoping I wouldn't have to use it. Wasn't I here to pick up a shawl?

The spider hissed and scrambled to strike my boss. Before it could take two steps, Bill swept his outstretched fingers to the right. Hangers and signs jumped off the rack and pelted the creature. Decorative vases and an umbrella stand followed. The spider scrambled for cover into the blackened corner. Its crimson pupils stared back at us.

"Are you done?" I shouted at Bill. "There are humans next door."

"They'll be fine," Bill drawled. "I've kept all the fun right here. Are you ready to talk now, Spider?"

The yatsukahagi hissed from the corner and its quivering fangs made a *click-clack* noise. A gravelly voice replied, "I bought the lamps as a part of a shipment from overseas."

A sliver of paper slid across the floor from the back. Bill snatched it.

"What is that?" I asked Bill as I hurried over to Wilhelm to check on him. The poor guy held his shirt over his bleeding shoulder.

"It's the manifest for the lamps," Bill explained. "Everything looks legit. Matter of fact, he got a pretty good deal from Brown Nose Associates in Germany." He sounded way too casual.

"Do you need help to apply pressure?" I asked.

"He'll be fine. Leave him be," Bill replied. "A good ass-kicking keeps kids nice and fresh."

"I'm eight-hundred and fifty years-old and he still sees me as a kid," Wilhelm grumbled.

Bill tossed the paper to the floor. "At eight-hundred-fifty, I could sell a human out of their shirt."

Once I was satisfied that Wilhelm wouldn't bleed to death —no thanks to Bill—I asked the spider about what I came here for. "I'm so sorry about what happened. Can I still get that silk shawl? The leprechaun told me he'd already paid for it."

An agitated series of clacks came from the corner. With my luck, the leprechaun probably underpaid. "Take it and leave. Your business is done here."

A delicate silk shawl arranged in tissue paper tumbled across the floor. The spider had even wrapped the package in a delicate red ribbon.

Without another word, Bill left. Wilhelm ran after him.

I picked up the parcel with a long sigh. "How much did Seamus pay for this?"

"Not enough," the spider grumbled. "But like many, I owe a debt to the leprechauns. With this deal, I'm paid in full."

"I am so sorry about this," I repeated as I left.

Once I was outside the door and back in the car, I blew out a sigh of relief. The OPEN sign was gone and a quickly scribbled note saying, *"closed for the day"* was adhered to the glass door.

I didn't dare glance in the back seat to see if Bill's apprentice bled all over my seats. I had bigger problems than my incessant OCD. To keep myself on track, I grabbed a blanket and first aid kit from the trunk.

When I climbed back in the car, I caught the rancid smell of burned flesh.

"What the hell are you two doing back there?" I barked.

"Oh, I just burned his stump," Bill said. "He'll grow another arm in a couple of days."

I tossed the first aid kit on the passenger seat floor. There went using that. I handed the blanket to Wilhelm. I bet he didn't expect to lose a limb when he signed up for the apprenticeship program.

"Did you find what you're looking for after all *that*?" I asked Bill.

"That thing is too weak to cause the problems at The

Bends," he replied. "Maybe someone poisoned those lamps after they arrived at the lightning bird's place."

"So was it the lightning bird?" I pulled away from Arachne's as fast as I could.

"Not necessarily." Bill rolled down the window to drive the smoke out of the car. "I know the guy. Horrible business-man, but he's got no beef with me."

"Those lamps are nothing but trouble." We were back on the main road, and I sagged against the steering wheel. "I just don't get it. Back at the lightning bird's place, I didn't smell anything off."

Bill slowly nodded. "I'd wager a half a buck he's seeing signs right about now."

"This is bad." I rubbed the beginning of an ache across my temple. "Any customer could've walked into the store and added the curse."

"What a horrible waste of resources," Wilhelm added. "Why make such mischief?"

"I've seen this kind of work before," my goblin employer said darkly. "With She Who Always Walks the Path gener-ating supernatural traffic, anyone could be behind this." He added, "Give me some time to do some digging before you do your fourth task with the leprechaun."

"Are you sure?" I replied. "I only have a month to get all this done."

"Yep. I'll have things wrapped up before your month is over." Bill gave me a genuine grin.

Did he find all this funny?

The goblin added, "The real fun begins once I find the culprit and *kill* them."

CHAPTER EIGHT

After four hours on the road, I was cranky and ready to hunt down a hare. On the way to The Bends, we stopped off at Archie's for some burgers. Poor Wilhelm ate his sandwich with one hand while Bill munched away on the opposite side of the back seat.

I considered having Wilhelm fill out an Occupational Safety and Health Administration form for a workplace accident and injuries, but I changed my mind. We had enough to worry about without bringing humans into the mix.

"Do you have a problem if I call Brenna over to check things out?" I asked Bill. "Would be nice to get her perspective on the curse."

Bill's shoulders lifted and fell. "Those spellcasters will be sniffing around sooner or later. Can't take a piss without one of them looking over my shoulder. I trust her more than most of them."

We returned to an empty store. As to be expected, Erica had closed the place down. I almost anticipated seeing August burst through the double doors, but no one appeared.

Matter of fact, even my goblin companions vanished after I entered the back office.

I shrugged and shot Brenna a quick text message. At least I didn't have to worry about finicky stock and clerks casting crazy spells. I found Erica at one of the desks going through the morning receipts. Rex had left for his lunch break.

"Did you learn anything?" she asked.

"Not much." I left a bag with burgers and fries next to her computer.

"Oh, thanks. Smells delish." She focused on the screen as her glossy pink manicured nails clicked on the keyboard.

I explained, in agonizing detail, everything I'd learned so far from the moment August was discovered dead up to the news from the spider. Gradually, Erica's flawless face changed from appalled to bitter.

"I can't believe August is dead," she breathed. "When I left last night, he was excited about re-arranging one of the armor displays." She slowly shook her head. "Do we need to do anything to contact his next of kin?"

Those were all questions I had to consider. "Right now, I don't know."

Now that I was safe and sound at work, I shot off a text to my mate. The pack might run into problems if others died like August. A killer could be out there, and I didn't have all the facts.

A half hour later, I got a message back from Brenna: *Can stop by after my shift this afternoon. Will be there around 3 p.m.*

I turned to Erica and explained my plan to dig for clues. "I'm going to see if I can find out what happened so far."

She opened the bag and grabbed one of the burgers. "Let me know if I can help."

"Thanks." Since the store was closed, we didn't have much to do.

First things first, I watched the camera footage from

inside the back office starting from one yesterday morning. Some chairs wheeled back and forth across the room, but not much else happened. By 3 a.m., Rex had shown up to begin his shift to pick up parcels and deliver them from the dock to the back office. From there, I increased the camera speed to show August arriving to help Rex sort through stock. Wilhelm showed up not long after. Several times Wilhelm and August spoke to each other, but around 7 a.m. an argument broke out between August and Rex. I hit pause. By that point, Erica stood behind me.

"What were they arguing about?" she whispered.

"Rex probably found out his true working hours," I surmised, "or that we use cheap toilet paper with the consistency of dried cornstalks."

I hit play and increased the volume to full. The men's voices blared from the computer speakers.

"Just tell me what to do!" Rex belted out. "I don't have time to remember your stupid work list."

"Stupid work list? I sent you an email last night."

"I'm not reading fifty fucking pages on how to sweep a floor. You gotta be kidding me."

"Mr. Chapman, if you don't mind me calling you Rex, I believe there's a misunderstanding here." August put his hands up and calmly approached Rex. "We'd hoped you'd read the booklet, but if you'd like on the job training—"

"Just tell me what to do."

August ran his fingers through his hair in frustration. "That's a *complete* waste of time. You have a work schedule. From three in the morning until five, you're supposed to take the boxes from the dock and arrange them over in the stock corner. They should be arranged alphabetically—"

"Again, why can't you tell me what I should do *right now?*" Rex was about ready to pop.

"Great, let me read the manual to you." August headed

over to the desk to fetch a thick binder. "During our interview you didn't say anything about not knowing how to read. But, then again, werewolves have been known to have lower intelligence." He leafed through the binder. "You didn't sound stupid over the phone."

Rex advanced toward August, his chest widening as a growl formed in his throat. His fist rose to strike before he took a step back. "You guys need to seriously loosen up your stupid rules."

"Whoa," Erica said. "August was about to meet the floor."

August didn't let up. "If you have any ideas, we have an employee suggestion box—"

"That's not what I mean," Rex said. "Look, I'm gonna go over there and bring in everything and you're going to help me sort it. We'll figure things out."

"Sounds good."

Rex left the back office and headed out. August stood there for a moment, perhaps valuing his life before he followed Rex. The two men went back and forth out of the shot as they grabbed the boxes off the loading dock. August kept a safe distance from Rex the whole time.

"Do you think August got in a fight with Rex later?" Erica asked.

"I don't know," I replied. "I wish I could see August's body again to see if he'd been badly beaten. I didn't notice any bruises or contusions."

"Any blood?" she asked.

"Not that I could see or smell. Goblin blood smells like… goblins. When I discovered his body, he didn't smell like much else."

"We really need to talk to Rex."

"That's obvious."

A couple hours later, Brenna pulled up to The Bends parking lot. I met her under the awnings on the side of the store. The earth witch wore a pair of cargo shorts, a white peasant blouse, and some sandals. I'd give my right paw to have her sunny disposition today.

"Thanks for coming," I said, gesturing for her to follow me inside.

"Sounded serious," she replied.

"It's more than serious at this point." I explained how August had been found dead, too.

"Geez. Is everyone else okay?"

"So far."

We walked past the wand display when a couple jumped out again. Brenna caught a stick in one hand while she flicked away another with her other hand. "You trying to get me to buy something?" she joked.

I snorted. "I wish the merchandise was that effective. For the past week, all sorts of weird stuff has happened. It's like there's some sort of interference with the...harmony of Bill's magic."

Brenna's nose wrinkled as if she smelled something bad. "There's a heaviness here—like it's humid. It's hard to describe. I feel it on my skin, in my lungs. It's everywhere."

"There's more. Let me show you the back dock and the roof." She followed me outside. From there, I pointed to the greenish spots on the roof.

"Got any ideas?" I asked. "Bill says it's a curse."

She used her hand to block out the afternoon sun as she peered upward. "It's a curse all right. And I've seen those spots somewhere else."

Oh, no. "Where?"

"Kramkar's place across the street."

"Shit." So the troll's store had it, too.

"Since we don't understand how the contagion is spread," she said, "I'll do some research with the respective guilds."

I held back a sigh. "What about the warlocks? Do you think they'll pop up once you start checking?"

Brenna patted my arm in sympathy. "I'll make sure this stays under the radar, but if the curse is spreading, I can't protect y'all."

It was never good when the warlocks got involved. Not too long ago, Sedgewick McGalleon, one of the representatives from the Warlock's Guild, had issued the South Toms River Pack a warning. His words echoed through my head as Brenna bid me a goodbye. *We'll be watching you and observing how you conduct yourselves in the future. Members from the Warlock's Guild will be responsible for enforcing this observation.*

At this point, my day could only get better.

~

As much as I wanted to go home and crash hard, I had to track down Rex. After he took his lunch break, he'd worked outside for a while, but I never saw him again. I considered waiting until tomorrow, but questioning him before the day ended seemed the best option. Since he always took on extra shifts during the holidays, I stopped at his other workplace, the Last Mark Bar and Grill off Dover Road. The likelihood of finding a couple pack members enjoying the holiday crowd was high.

The parking lot was packed and it took me a while to find a spot. Fifteen agonizing minutes later, I entered the bar. My ears rang from the cacophony of laughter, clinking glasses, and the melodic wailing of an electric guitar. The air was thick with the mingled scents of sweat and cheap beer. Looked like this was the place for everyone to celebrate the Fourth. Bright lights twinkled at the bar. Over there a bunch of patrons slammed down berry sparkler cocktails and watched a New York Yankees baseball game.

My eyes scanned the bright room. It was hard to find Rex in the crowd. Dancers even filled the party floor as a rock cover band was in full swing, their rendition of a classic rock tune vibrating through the floorboards under my feet. My gaze settled on Rex. He bustled about in one of the far corners, deftly balancing a tray loaded with empty glasses and plates. Not once did he look in my direction. Was he still upset after I saw him working here not too long ago? Back then, the manager gave him a hard time in front of everyone.

As he began cleaning up a large, recently vacated ten-seater table, I seized the opportunity to speak to him.

"Rex, we need to talk," I said, raising my voice to be heard over the din.

Three women holding lime margaritas squeezed between us. "Hey, Rex!" one of the brunettes shouted.

"You working late tonight?" another purred as she leaned in close to him.

"Maybe," he said with a false grin.

After they left, he turned to me, resigned, and set down the tray. "What do you want?"

"August died this morning, and I wondered if you know anything," I asked.

Rex's eyes widened momentarily before he swallowed hard and shook his head. "I didn't kill him, Nat. I swear."

I crossed my arms. "Tell me what you know."

"I got to work at three in the morning," Rex began. "August was busy doing something in another room. When the delivery came, we spent the whole morning unloading. After we wrapped up things around seven, he disappeared."

"I saw you two arguing on the security feed."

Rex's cheeks flushed with anger. "Yeah, we argued. August is a prick." He stacked the plates into his tray. "He gave me a detailed schedule like I'm too stupid to figure shit out. I can't stand those goblins, but I'd never kill them."

Rex spoke the truth. His scent said as much.

"Thanks," I said. "But we need to figure out who killed August. Keep your eyes open and let me know if you see or hear anything."

Rex nodded. "You got it."

With that, I escaped the bar, wishing I had fewer questions and more answers.

CHAPTER NINE

Almost a week had passed and I had nineteen days left to complete Seamus' tasks. The heat levels rose, dragging the Jersey countryside through a barbecue pit. Bill had yet to give me the go-ahead to attempt the fourth task from Seamus.

I was outside, yet again rearranging things after Rex had taken it upon himself to start barking out orders once August had died. August had been the pushier one between the apprentices and once that gap formed, Rex slid his annoying self in place.

Two days ago, I tore apart the back office for some masking tape. Yesterday I had to hunt down a customer's box, namely the box containing a bird's nest for that pushy harpy, Mrs. Kite. Lo and behold, Wilhelm had replaced the label and Rex just tossed it wherever he pleased. No organization. No planning. Just a hot mess dumped in my already full lap.

I finished the tasks, then turned on the outdoor fans under the awnings. A stranger appeared off the sidewalk. He hadn't gotten out from a car, nor had he walked up from one of the opposite lots. He simply materialized on the sidewalk and approached me. He wore a long, black overcoat, along with a black bowler hat and shiny leather shoes. Those clothes were far too warm for this weather. His glamour was well reinforced, and only his iron-like scent revealed I had a powerful goblin before me.

"I'm Mr. Hässlicheschuhe," the man said in a rough Bronx accent. "I'm with the New York district's Goblin Apprenticeship Program."

"Good afternoon, mister," I attempted to say his name and word-spaghetti spilled out. I extended my hand for a shake, but he ignored it. Suited me just fine.

"You may call me, Mr. Sells-Ugly-Shoes. We received a report a week ago from a Mr. Wilhelm Löchrigesleder about the death of Mr. Bill's associate. Were you aware of that report?"

Mr. Bill? Didn't Bill have a last name like all goblins?

"Yes, I discovered August's body."

"Oh, so you're the one who found Mr. Modeschmuck. According to the report, Mr. Bill had *found* him."

"Bill took care of the body. I just found him, that's all."

The goblin pulled out a notepad and a tiny pencil, and he began scribbling on it. He paused for a moment, cracked his neck with a jerk of his head to the right, and he kept going. I cringed from the sound.

"According to the report, Mr. Modeschmuck had been murdered. Is that correct?" the goblin asked.

"I'm not sure. I didn't get a chance to examine August before Bill took care of him."

"Darn shame. According to the apprentice program policy, applicants may be dismembered or gutted, but death is not allowed."

So evisceration is acceptable but not death. Bat shit madness.

Mr. Sells-Ugly-Shoes continued. "Are you aware of the fact Mr. Bill has two strikes against him, and he won't be allowed to have any more apprentices?"

"No, I wasn't aware of that. Bill brought on these apprentices without any input from me. What are the consequences when you have too many strikes?" Wow, what had Bill done over the years?

"It's not the Goblin Apprenticeship Program's policy to divulge what happens when a site kills off their apprentices, but I can tell you, Mr. Bill is in big trouble."

"That's not good."

"No, it isn't, Ms. Stravinsky." His head jerked to the left with a hard *crack, crack*. "Is Mr. Bill available?"

"Bill hasn't been around for the last couple of days." I fished out my phone. "I can call him right now and he can explain everything."

At least I had a reason to force Bill to show up, but after a few calls, Bill didn't pick up. An emergency text didn't work either.

Mr. Sells-Ugly-Shoes stared me down, his pencil hovering over his notepad. "Mr. Bill needs to produce evidence as to what happened in his apprentice's accidental death. If that evidence isn't produced, the Goblin Apprenticeship Program will revoke Mr. Bill's license to sell goods. After that, he'll have to close this establishment."

CHAPTER TEN

Night arrived, and with it, I dreamt. As of late, I've been running through the forest, searching for something I couldn't find, but tonight, I ran away from Diana. Her voice carried on the wind. *You know the weight of the leash connecting you to me, and soon enough I will yank the chain. And you will kneel. You will beg for the scraps I feed my animals,* Diana said. *Unless you wish to run from me, and I hope you do.*

The Goddess added, *For our struggle will become the Hunt of the Ages. A feast for my soul. And at the conclusion of that Endless Night, you will surrender and be mine forevermore.*

My legs pumped and my arms clawed at the air. The forest had no end. No beginning. Branches smacked my face as I struggled to fill my lungs. Each breath made the collar around my neck draw tighter. With each step, my body— both human and wolf—was reminded I couldn't run forever. Sooner or later, these muscles, my heart in particular, would stop. And after that, I'd have to confront my enemies, both internal and external.

The collar around my neck jerked back. The crown of my head slammed to the ground. A hand grasped my hair and tugged upward, hard enough to draw my piercing scream.

I woke at that moment.

"No…" In the land between reality and dreams, I'd said that word. My throat was raw as I shuddered. I brushed my fingers against my collarbone finding nothing there.

Thorn wrapped his arms around me as a midnight-born rainstorm tapped against the roof. "You're safe." His voice was groggy with sleep, but the strength in his arms reassured me. Quieted me.

He said the words again, even drawing his leg over mine. He rained kisses over my scalp—which still ached as if I'd truly fought Diana.

I tried to sleep, but every time my eyes began to close, the wolf within nipped at me to stay awake. There'd be no rest tonight. Once I knew my beloved had fallen asleep, I slipped out of his arms and trudged over to the kitchen. My mom had left the fixings for some sandwiches, so I made myself a huge pastrami sandwich, grabbed a TV tray, then settled into the living room on the Lazy-Z-Boy. The recliner's cushions hugged me close and the TV remote was right there. Time for some Home Shopping Network.

After an hour or two, I became an advertiser's dream. Up late and itching to distract myself, I whipped out my credit card and spent the night chatting with telemarketers.

～

Hours later, I drained a carafe of coffee with two shots of espresso. Anything less and I couldn't call myself functional.

After I received a long hug from Thorn, I staggered to work. The heavy rain left the roads slick and drivers darted from lane to lane like anxious rabbits. Somehow, I got to work without a mishap. Bill showed up as I started the morning shift at The Bends. He strode in with a flickering glamour and revealed haggard features across his glossy green cheeks. Compared to the other goblins, Bill had wiry tufts of white hair and lines stretched across his scowling face. Guess he was his usual chipper self.

"Glad you showed up. Things are bad," I said.

"No shit."

"A Goblin Apprenticeship Program inspector came by yesterday. He asked about August."

A wave of emotions, none of them tactful, crossed Bill's face. He spat out a curse in German, then he strode over to his desk and turned on his computer.

Oh, no, he wasn't gonna walk away from me again. "Don't we need to do something about this? The inspector said we needed evidence as to how August died, or else he'll shut down The Bends."

"I got this." Bill took a seat. "You just mind the store and find out what's going on with the curse."

"Speaking of the curse, did you find anything? Did you figure out who's behind all of this?"

Bill stared at the computer screen. An expenses Excel sheet reflected off his glasses. For a moment, he appeared human. He almost reminded me of a salaryman coming off an overtime shift.

"I still don't know what's wrong," he said sternly. "This shit is like a bad jock itch. One scratch and the infection is all over your damn hands."

Ugh. He could've used any example to make his point. Truly.

The back office doors opened, and Rex strode in. He turned around to motion for Wilhelm to back up a delivery truck right up to the back dock. From there, they unloaded boxes.

"I think we should close today," I said carefully. "I managed to hire some supernatural temp workers, but we can't keep this up forever. Sooner or later, the human customers will get suspicious."

"Then we'll do private shopping parties. I can send messages out to the various guilds and supernatural organizations. Maybe we can make it a day party kind of thing. You know, we'll give the folks some wine and sell them all sorts of shiny things." Bill said all of this with a straight face, as if anyone could strike up a partnership with a winery.

"We can try that," I said carefully, "but I don't feel comfortable leaving the investigation in your hands. This problem looks bigger than you can manage, Bill."

"Then I should help," Rex said.

"That's a fantastic idea," Bill said, his face brightening. "You and Natalya can go out and search the shops within a twenty-mile radius. Find out if any of them are poisoned, and which shops specifically *aren't* yet."

Rex nodded, quite pleased with himself, while I stood there with a straight face.

"If we're organizing shopping trips," I said, "shouldn't I stay here to handle that?"

"Didn't you just say this is all bigger than I can manage?" Bill knew very well what he was doing to me, and if he weren't vulnerable, I would've clawed the smile off his face.

"I can do this on my own and report back before midnight," Rex said smoothly. "She'll just slow me down."

Here we go again. If I had the opportunity to choose a tracker, Rex would've been last on my list. After all the attacks on the pack, he *still* couldn't track a carousel horse.

"Even if you to split up, you still need each other." Bill

folded his arms and a knowing look passed between Rex and Bill.

"Yeah, I can't see the infected parts." Rex sighed.

"Then we have a plan, people." Bill started typing again. "You two get to work while I learn about rich lady winery stuff."

CHAPTER ELEVEN

Rex left me behind on his way to his truck. By the time he got to his, I was halfway to mine. When he opened his door, I hesitated. We couldn't work like this. The searing heat from my *babushka's* glare for letting my feelings get in the way of my job scorched my backside.

"Even the most bitter fruits taste sweet to someone," I heard grandma say. "Go to him. Be the better person like your *dedushka*. Your grandfather always tried his best."

I gave up on the Altima and ran over to Rex's vehicle. When I tapped on the window, he glanced up in surprise. He blinked a couple times before he unlocked the door. Without saying another word, I got inside and strapped on my seatbelt. One thing I had to give Rex, he kept a pristine car. I expected him to be messy like Thorn, but the surfaces shined with leather polish. Even the interior leather had no rips and stains. At least, Rex loved *something*.

"Is there a store you want to check out first?" See, I knew how to be a peacekeeper.

"I dunno. That infection could be anywhere. Don't you

shop too much?" He laughed not with me but at me. "For all we know, you're spreading your cooties all over town."

One step forward. Two steps back.

I blinked and imagined sunshine and puppies.

After shoving my pride into a tree shredder, I replied. "Brenna told me Kramkar's shop is infected. I haven't confirmed if Archie's or the bakery had problems. We should go there."

"Okay."

With a plan—somewhat—in place, we headed off to Archie's. The restaurant hadn't opened yet for customers, but I could imagine the grill fired up and burgers sizzling on top. Too bad we couldn't eat.

Once we got there, Rex found a parking spot and took in the building with the engine running. Did he plan to get out and *actually* look?

"Shouldn't we go inside?" I asked.

"Naw."

I grabbed the handle. He still didn't get out. Screw this.

I left to do a sweep. Not long after, Rex killed the engine and followed. Any minute now he'd have sage wisdom to give, but he remained silent with his accusations, while I sidestepped the puddles and circled Archie's from the front to the back.

To fill the painful silence, I spoke. "How are you holding up at work? Is there anything you need?"

"I'm fine."

I tugged a bit harder to get more than a single or two-word response. "Is there anything you need? Wilhelm tends to get pushy with the staff."

Rex checked behind the dumpster off the parking lot. The front looked good. "Bill pays shit, but he's willing to work around my evening shifts."

A rotten aroma wafted from the slimy green container. I

took a step back. He definitely took one for the team. "That's good to hear. Things have been crazy."

"What I do know is the last janitor got a bum deal."

"Quinton?"

"Yeah. Must've been a stand-up dude 'cause you guys didn't give a shit about him."

My forehead furrowed. "What do you mean?"

"Have you been in the little closet where he keeps the cleaning supplies?"

"Not really." I recalled standing in the doorway to the necromancer's domain, but I never entered the windowless crypt. Even the brightest light in the back office didn't penetrate the blackened corners. For all I knew, one of his zombie minions guarded the cleaning cart.

Rex moved on to check the business sign off the road, then we headed to the dark-purple building. "He has this tiny calendar—one of those cheap ones you get from the charities—and he tracked everyone's birthdays."

"I didn't know that."

"Yeah, he had a life outside work." Rex gave me a genuine smile. "He loves a bunch of goth bands like The Cure. Whenever there was a concert nearby, he went."

"I never knew." I glanced through the window of the burger joint, examining the red booths and familiar advertisements on the walls. When I stopped by at Archie's, I always found Jake and Misty joking or having fun. Even Harold, the owner, loved a good prank once in a while. The team had a lot more camaraderie than we had at The Bends.

"I've always enjoyed my work," I admitted. "I love antiques. I truly do, but I don't like managing people."

"I love telling people what to do."

I snorted. *Of course you do, pal.*

Rex tapped the purple bricks. Everything seemed sound. "I might not be as much of a straight arrow like you, but I do know when someone deserves more respect. I might not *admit* it, but I do notice it."

We checked the building twice, but after finding nothing, we moved on to the fairy place. The only supernatural bakery within South Toms River had the most delicious aromas. Grandma Lasovskaya loved their funnel cakes while Dad often fished coins from his pocket for their buttery scones. Even Aggie always scoped out their sales.

We only had to pull up in front of the building for me to see the curse had spread. The stenciled name of the shop had faded from its normally pristine shine, and the smoke drifting from the chimney had a strange glimmer. That smoke came from the ovens. Did that mean the food was cursed, too? The thought soured my stomach.

Over the last couple of days, I hadn't changed my shopping habits. Maybe some of this was my fault. Maybe I should've walked out of the lightning bird's shop empty-handed. I couldn't help but shudder at the thought of passing on a good deal.

I opened the car door and tried to bury my darkening thoughts. If I wanted to make things better, I had to get to work. I could lick my wounds later.

Like any other morning, we were greeted inside by one of the clerks, a fairy named Esmeralda. She smiled at us from behind the counter as she helped a couple preorder a wedding cake with all the fixings. While I waited for her, Rex stalked through the seating area, checking behind two tables and over the counter.

The fairy wrapped up her consultation and turned to me. "Hey, Nat. What can I help you with?"

I slid closer to the counter and couldn't help but notice their display for an upcoming promotion. Glossy pink script read: *"There's nothing sweeter than our Scrumptious Cakes collectibles."* A beautiful set of glass red velvet cakes with delightful grins and bright eyes had every bit of the Christmas morning happiness I loved.

"Like those?" she piped up. "Every slice of cake you buy is an entry into our Scrumptious Cakes Figurine giveaway."

Those fairies charmed me every time. Even the prizes for the upcoming giveaway winked at me.

Rex leaned on the corner and offered his award-winning grin.

"Hey, Essie, how are you doing? Haven't seen you in a while." The man's machismo practically elbowed me out of the way. "Have you noticed anything weird around here?"

"Not that I've noticed." Esmeralda's eyes jerked in my direction. "We've had a lot more customers than usual, but we've been running a sale."

I knew for a fact Rex rarely came in here. He probably only stopped in when someone else was with him. Not everyone frequented the bakery. Their prices leaned toward the expensive side, but anyone who'd sampled one of their cakes would say they were practically magical.

"Do you mind if I take a look around?" Rex asked. "We'll be in and out of that gorgeous blonde hair of yours in no time."

"Umm, sure," she replied.

I held back a chortle. Rex couldn't see Esmeralda's true form. He saw a blonde with rosy full cheeks and generous hips, but I glimpsed underneath the glamour and saw her shinier, lankier form. Her height met my shoulders, and she had wiry red, not blonde hair.

"And while we're looking around, can I get some donuts for my grandma?" I added. "She loves to eat them with Aunt Olga."

Rex shifted to leave. "Stay here then. I'll scope out the joint by myself. If I notice anything, I *might* bring you over."

The word "might" sure felt like "not gonna happen," but I still planned to follow him, nonetheless.

Rex left the shop, and the moment the door shut, Esmeralda's face twisted with disapproval.

"What's his deal?" She stooped to snag the prettiest pink donuts from the display. I dropped two bucks into the tip jar.

"If you find out, let me know," I replied. "Rex is working at The Bends now, and I can only stand him in small doses."

"I thought once he started taking care of his brothers, he'd grow up some."

"Me, too."

"His family is cool. When we have expired food, his brother Melvin loves to stop by at the end of the day. Rex always waits in the car down the street like it's shameful." She pursed her glossy lips and carefully arranged the donuts into a carton. With a wink, she added two blushing gingerbread cookies.

"Yeah," I replied. "I can imagine it's hard for him to accept help. I didn't know they stopped by for the free bread. I hope they're using the food pantry down in Toms River."

"I don't know, but they should. Ever since we came from the Old Country, my family has always helped those in need. If good-natured folk—" she glanced up at me with a mischievous smile, "leave out a cup of tea with honey on their back doorstep, one of my uncles leaves them food, too."

I grinned. "So that legend is true."

"Depends on the time of the year, and if one of my uncles is in town. I hope things improve for Rex and his brothers. I've lived here a long time and I'm older than I look. I remember when Rex and his brothers were much younger. He had a rough childhood, and his parents let those poor boys run all over town."

I nodded with sympathy, recalling when my father

worked extra shifts to support my family. He dirtied his paws in Atlantic City to make sure we ate.

Esmeralda continued, wrapping up the transaction when I handed her my credit card. "I've seen Rex working around town when I've made deliveries. He should be exhausted at this point. Those other two aren't pulling their weight."

Right then, Rex appeared behind the glass front door. He mouthed the words, "Didn't find anything."

"Can he hear us?" I asked.

"The whole place is soundproof," Esmeralda explained. "Also, we have too many supernaturals coming in and out. All he can hear is that annoying supermarket music."

"Well, he said he didn't find anything on the outside and you said you haven't seen anything on the inside, but may I check out your kitchen to see if I can find the curse? I noticed your smoke had a weird tinge do it."

Her face drained of its shimmery colors. "That doesn't sound good. Our kitchen is very clean. Uncle would be upset if we had any dark magic in there."

I turned around and motioned for Rex to return inside.

He sauntered in. "Why are we checking in here? I already did a sweep outside, and we still got a bunch of other places to check." He threw a glare at my donuts.

"I'm just going to do a quick sweep of the kitchen," I said, leaving him behind as I joined Esmeralda. Rex had no choice but to follow.

"Our bakery looks pretty small from the outside," Esmeralda explained to me, "but we use magic to hide our state-of-the-art facility."

I followed the fairy down a short hallway with two doorways to the right. One led to a storage room, a very tidy one. The other one was an office. Two fairies processed receipts and invoices at L-shaped desks.

One even rang out, "Hey, Natalya! Hope your grandma loves the donuts!"

"They won't last long," I replied.

So far, I hadn't caught anything amiss or any signs that the curse had taken hold in the bakery. At the end of the hallway, we reached the baking room with three industrial sized ovens. A winding conveyor belt led from dough processing units to the ovens. On the other side of the room, nimble fairies manned a prep station to add custard and fruit fillings to the pastries.

The whole place smelled like heaven on earth.

"In most facilities, you wouldn't be able to be in here without proper clothing and nets over your hair," she explained, "but our magic keeps most allergens and other pesky bugs away. Do you see any problems?"

Rex remained at the doorway while I followed the conveyor belt closer to the middle oven. Delicate cookies, ready to be browned to a crisp rolled down the line. I could practically taste them, imagining the delight on my family's faces as they ate. The closer I got to the oven, the more my stomach formed knots. I couldn't ignore the suspicious smoke.

All I had to do was peek inside. A bright green sparkle danced among the flames.

Esmeralda must've read my face. "You see it, don't you?"

"I'm so sorry. You're infected with the curse we found at The Bends. It's in your ovens."

Every fairy on the work floor scrambled over. They threw questions at me.

"How much is it?" one man asked.

"Is it in all the ovens?" another said.

"What caused this?"

They practically circled me now. "How come we can't see it?" the first fairy asked.

"I'm so sorry," I said as loudly as possible. "A couple of days ago, we noticed the infection. Rest assured, Bill has been trying to find a cure."

"Why are we learning this now?" A fairy stepped forward with an air of authority. That had to be Esmeralda's Uncle Johannes. He didn't stand taller than the others, but he had his hands on his hips and the way he held his head back stated his rank. "For the past four centuries, I've never had a curse."

"We're notifying everyone." My voice didn't sound confident anymore. "I can see the curse through my goblin magic. Otherwise, I wouldn't know you had it either."

"So this is a goblin curse?" Johannes asked.

"I don't know," I admitted. "I'm so sorry, I don't know."

Long ago, I learned to never promise the fairy folk I'd do *anything*. Unfulfilled promises resulted in consequences, and I rather liked breathing and moving.

From the other side of the room, I caught Rex's smug expression. He conveniently *stayed* over there while I took not only the heat from the bakery kitchen's oven, but the ire from the pissed off fairies.

Over the years, Rex had proven again and again that he'd always been on Team Rex. He floated to the top of turbulent waters while everyone else drowned in the wake of his selfishness.

CHAPTER TWELVE

A couple years ago, before Thorn returned as the prodigal son to lead the South Toms River Pack, Rex had consistently played a part in ostracizing me from everyone—including my own family.

I could still hear, and feel, the impact from the words he'd said to Thorn after my husband had returned to town: "What are you doing talking to her anyway?" Rex had said. "She's not pack anymore."

As the alpha female now, one would think I would've moved on, but old wounds were fissures. Over time they strengthened or weakened. You see, you can never forget the pain someone else inflicts on you. As time passes the feeling retreats until the memory flares up again, as breathtaking as it was before.

Not long after Thorn left and disappeared for a long time, my family tried to console me. I resembled a broken piece of china, but I went to therapy and put *myself* back together.

After that, the depth of Rex's cruelty had no end. Every couple of months, he'd drive past my parents' house, either stopping by to eat dinner or rolling by so I could glimpse his smug smile. Every grin had the taint of victory. His over mine. Thorn was gone, leaving the second-in-command position open, and I'd returned broken.

His struggle for power had really ramped up during high school. I'd roamed the halls, going from class to class watching Thorn from afar while Rex played the role of Thorn's best friend. When Thorn joined the football team for fun, Rex did, too, but Rex didn't hold back his strength and intimidated the human kids. Whenever Thorn ate out with his brother Will and his dad Farley, Rex was there, laughing at the former pack leader's horrible jokes.

Now that I think about it, knowing the present and the past, those dinners were probably the only time Rex had a father figure in his life. Why go home to find an empty fridge and non-existent parents? But then again, he could've gone home and made sure his brothers ate. Instead of acting out and following Thorn around, he could've gotten a part-time job to help his family. Hell, he could've left—anything to disrupt the status quo instead of just…existing.

Instead, Rex had carefully positioned himself with Farley. The former pack leader believed in him, even encouraging him to apply to the University of Pittsburgh to go to college with Thorn.

Around that time in the early fall of our senior year, I'd lived in the high school library after classes. The librarians, bless them, had let students stay until closing time. Every day, I took over a single table in the corner and tackled my homework and diligently built up a list of notes for my college application essay.

One day Rex showed up, fresh from a shower after football practice. He walked through the door and every single student briefly took him in. Like Thorn, Rex had that effect on others—until he opened his mouth.

"You're Natalya, right?" he asked me.

He knew my damn name. We'd seen each other all the time at pack gatherings.

"Yeah." I scribbled a couple of words, hoping he'd take the hint to move on about his business.

Rex rested his still wet hands against the side of the table —right next to my work. A couple drops dampened my papers' corners. I shifted the papers to the side.

He said, "The other day, I heard you tell the guidance counselor that you're trying to get into UPitt."

"And?" I whispered too low for a human to hear, but clear enough for a werewolf.

"I'm trying to get in too," he replied, not bothering to whisper. "I say we team up to write those essays." He leaned over to peek at my notes. "You've already done the research. I can give you tips to win 'em over."

Over the next five minutes, much to the librarian's ire, Rex spoke highly of his writing skills and his extra-curricular activities. He'd *donate* his spare time to help me write a great piece. By the way, I had no plans to add a steaming pile of bullshit to my work.

"So how about it?" he pressed. "After this, you can come with me to Archie's. I'm meeting Thorn there."

"I don't know…" He didn't know I liked Thorn, but he *did* know I didn't roll with the cool kids.

"Just give me a chance." He slipped into the seat across from me. "I heard some guy say he found a lot of great advice in some business book. Said it was called *How to Win New Customers?*"

"And?"

"Well, go get it. The guy's last name is Porter." He pointed to the non-fiction bookshelves. "Take a look and you'll see what I'm talking about."

I hesitated, then got up to search for the book. Murmurs floated through the room as I scanned the shelves. Rex never set foot in here, unless he was trailing after Thorn. Soon enough, I grabbed the book. When I returned, the notes for my essay were gone. Rex had beat a hasty retreat with his prize. Not a single person had seen his covert departure. Even me.

He never admitted or apologized for what he did.

That next spring, I learned how things when down. A couple gossiping students whispered that Thorn had gotten in, but Rex hadn't. And after learning the news, he stormed around the school showing his ass to everyone.

A few days later, Rex even managed to get the pack leader on his side. During a pack outing at the park, Farley griped, "Why didn't you *tell* Natalya to write it for you?"

"I'd never do that," Rex said smoothly. "She's a nobody. Why would I let a barely beta female touch my work?"

He spoke those words loud enough for any pack member within earshot to hear. I promised myself to never trust him again, but as Rex tried to rise in the ranks, he pulled down anyone in his way. Me included.

Now that I knew his true nature, I refused to be one of Rex's so-called victims. The back-and-forth had to end, and even if Rex didn't change, my reactions to him had to.

The workday never seemed to end with Rex. As we'd promised Bill, we checked every supernatural mart from the north to south. On most days, a shopaholic tour would leave me drunken with glee, but if I saw another clearance sign, I'd lose it. When we arrived at The Bends, I couldn't wait to jump in my car and hightail it home. To my surprise, a familiar face waited next to the Altima.

"Hey, you," Thorn said.

I couldn't resist smiling before I replied, "Hey, you."

"I brought you some food from Archie's." He tossed over a bag with two burgers and fries.

I'd already eaten at Archie's twice this week, but I grabbed the bag and swooped in for a hug. He pressed his lips against the crown of my head and breathed deep. The world could come crashing down on me and I knew he'd be there. Thorn didn't let me go when my arms fell. Almost as if he knew I needed someone to hold me up right now.

"How did it go with Rex?" he asked.

I probably still smelled like Rex and his car's lemony freshness. "Took forever." While I ate a couple of fries, I explained why we had to search all the supernatural shops.

"What about the Daltons' butcher shop? Do they need to watch out?"

The Dalton family were pack members and they'd recently gone through a tough period after losing their daughter to the Frost Giant's wolf.

"Their shop isn't enchanted so they should be fine."

He wrapped an arm around my shoulder and nudged for me to keep eating. My mate's body was relaxed, but I smelled fear hidden beneath his steady demeanor.

"What's on your mind?" I asked slowly.

"Not what, who." He didn't have to say her name. Her presence practically followed us from our bed to our workplaces.

"Yeah." I said the word with a long exhale.

"Can we run away from this problem?"

"Run where? Another universe? 'Cause we're talking godlike powers here."

His brow furrowed. "What about the wizard? Has he said anything?"

"Nick is busy at medical school. I'm on my own."

"Are you sure about that?" He asked those words carefully.

I didn't want to bring Nick into any of this. A wizard facing an army was one thing, but a goddess? Nick had shifted the heavens and harmed himself for me. This fight was beyond mortals and spellcasters.

"I don't know." I couldn't lie to Thorn.

"What if I take your place?"

"Oh, hell no."

He turned to face me and tilted my chin up. Our eyes met and his pain bubbled to the surface. "Do you think I'd stand by and let this happen to you?"

"Mevelyn already *sacrificed* herself for me. I'm not letting you do the same." I wanted to cry so bad it hurt, but I sucked in a breath. "I gave everything to save you back in Russia. I will never let you get in harm's way ever again."

"Doesn't the same apply to me?"

I jerked my chin away. He couldn't see me like this, even if my body, my damn heart, conveyed how much I was scared.

"When that *bitch* shows up, we're out of here." He pulled me into his arms and I rested my cheek against his chest. His heartbeat thrummed with a familiar rhythm. "You're not giving up on me. If she wants to hunt us, we'll give her a fight she'll never forget."

CHAPTER THIRTEEN

Nothing could ruin this Sunday. Especially with the rising sun casting a heavenly glow on the breakfast buffet my mom prepared this morning. Thorn and I had arrived early at my parents' house to greet Grandma and bask in the smells. After kissing Grandma Lasovskaya's wrinkled, yet warm cheek, I raided the sugar-dusted *ponchiki* balls. Thorn chuckled and headed to the garage to say hi to my dad. Nobody protested—not even Mom—when I took a generous helping of millet porridge. With a cheesy grin, I even drizzled honey and some blueberries on top.

At least once a week, my rambunctious Russian family had breakfast, lunch, or dinner together—especially since my mom loved to cook.

Grandma giggled from her seat next to the kitchen table. "Tastes perfect, no?"

"Like always," I replied.

On the other side of the kitchen, Mom hummed as she lovingly ladled drippings on the breakfast ham in the oven. It was like watching one of Aggie's favorite shows, *The Great*

British Bake-Off. Whether Mom baked, broiled, or fried the meat, she had wholesome written all over her.

Through the kitchen window, I spied a car pulling up. Aggie got out of the driver's seat and strolled up to the house. Briefly, our gazes connected through the window. I half expected her to turn around and leave. Over five days had passed since I sent her a text message asking about eating dinner together. And two days since I sent over a pic of the donuts I'd bought grandma.

My best friend hadn't replied to a single message.

Every now and then, when I peeked at the text message app, I caught three dots fluttering, an indicator she was typing a message, but she never replied.

Agatha stuffed her hands into her blue jean pockets and took her time, but eventually she joined the Stravinskys in the kitchen. Usually, Aggie had a plate of fixings before anyone could give her one. Today, she waited on the edge. My younger cousins roamed like a wayward pack, lost in a game of freeze tag.

"Either eat or get out," Mom snapped. "Do you want to get in my oven?"

The children scattered. The back door banged and sneakered feet squeaked on the linoleum floor.

Now that I didn't have to call a raid party to clear a path to the table, I sat with my breakfast. Not long after, Aggie got hers. She plopped down beside me.

"Morning." I tried to keep my tone casual.

"Hey." Using her fork, Aggie scooped the runny eggs on her toast. She opened her mouth wide and inhaled a massive bite.

"I've sent you some texts," I said. "Did you get them?"

She stopped mid-chew. "Yeah."

"Everything okay?"

"Yes…" Two quick chews. "Nope."

"Are you upset about what I said back in New York?" Might as well get it out.

"Do we have to talk about this right now?"

"I believe we should. It's not good for us to circle around the subject."

"I'm not circling around it—I'm trying to figure out a way *through* it."

I rolled the *ponchiki* balls from one side of my plate to the other in annoyance. "This is *much* bigger than you and me. I don't want—"

"Sitting around and waiting for the dog shit to fly isn't my style."

"No, it never has been. Brenna told me you've been asking the powerful New York packs for help."

"That and more. I'm not gonna let that bitch just show up and…" She opened her mouth to say more, but her thin lips sealed into a grim straight line.

Mom came up behind her and squeezed her shoulder. "You're a good friend, Aggie."

"Have any of you made any plans?" she asked softly.

Grandma leaned forward with her hand and reached across the table. Aggie quickly stood to rest her hand against Grandma's.

"My family, the Lasovskayas, could never decide on anything," she began to say in Russian. I translated for her. She continued with, "But the Stravinskys have always had iron in their bones. Like my boy Fyodor and his father, Natalya will rise to the occasion. I know you worry for her."

She rubbed the top of Aggie's larger hand. "When the time comes, we will strike."

"We will strike!" Uncle Boris repeated. He toasted Grandma with his morning whiskey.

A chorus of hurrahs erupted around the table. Even my younger cousins roared from the back door.

Warmth filled my chest and my throat dried. To keep myself from crying, I feigned a smile and downed the rest of my tea.

I'd give everything for these loud, outspoken people. Anything.

My phone dinged with another message and the slippery feeling down my spine said it all. I probably had the next mission from Seamus.

The message read:

> Hey, Nat. I can call you that since we're good friends, right? My associate, a Mr. Jasper McSteed has a special hammer I need for a customer. Due to an old family…feud, Mr. McSteed doesn't want to sell me the goods. I've transferred the necessary funds into your bank account. Help a leprechaun out and buy the hammer from my tommyknocker friend.

I'm his…friend? Eww. I wiped off my phone's screen as if he'd soiled it. And how did he find my bank account number? I take that back. *Days can be ruined.* Especially when a lowdown leprechaun got in the last word.

~

A small garage sale on the way to work brightened my morning until I ended my half-day shift at The Bends. Much to my surprise, Rex waited for me in the parking lot.

As much as I wanted to escape, Rex leaned against my car. Maybe if I turned around and worked for a bit longer, he'd forget about me.

"Is something going on?" I asked.

"I overheard you talking to Bill about taking the afternoon off to buy something else for the leprechaun."

Werewolf hearing seemed to always get me in trouble. This morning I'd had no trouble securing the afternoon off since Bill had planned a private wand party for a bunch of wind witches. Erica would host the party, the clerks would help serve the customers, and in the end, I'd have time to buy the hammer from Mr. McSteed.

"And why are you here?" I asked.

"Thorn told me to keep an eye on you. He's trying to find where Diana is hiding out."

I sighed. The goddess didn't like trespassers. "When I see him—"

"He'll be careful. Trust me. He knows not to get too close." Rex got into my car before I could protest. "You got that next task, right? Was that why you were checking out the address for a hardware store in Silverton? I know the area. I went to college up there."

As much as I didn't want Thorn to make such a dangerous decision, I couldn't control him. As the pack leader, his role was to protect not only me, but everyone else, too. What I hoped was he wouldn't have to use werewolf magic to protect himself. So far, I'd managed to avoid using Old Magic. For now.

Since I had little choice in the matter, Rex and I drove up the Parkway toward Silverton. I hadn't been to this area much, even though the small town was only a couple of minutes away from South Toms River. Like any river township, Silverton had marinas and houses lining Silver Bay. I rolled down the window and the heat seeped inside, but I welcomed the sounds of children playing and lawnmowers chugging along. Briefly, as we passed the homes and businesses along the Parkway, I felt like it was any other day until I noticed I was low on gas.

A werewolf can't remember everything, I reminded myself.

Before we could head up to Silverton, I stopped at a gas

station. Right across the street, I spotted the sign for nearby Ocean City College. A long time ago, I would've gone here if I hadn't gotten into UPitt. Dad had even taken me up here and we walked around.

"You'll save money if you go here instead of one of those big American schools," he'd said. "Staying at home with your family and commuting is best. Kids these days can't wait to leave."

Yes, I did end up leaving, but I returned home, too.

I pulled up to the gas pump. When the clerk, a woman with short, dirty blonde hair strode up to us, Rex stiffened.

I quickly surmised she was a rogue without a pack.

"Hey, how's it going?" She smiled and averted her eyes respectfully. "How many gallons?"

"Fill it up all the way. I've got a lot of driving to do." Beside me, I couldn't help but catch Rex shift to face away from the attendant.

That didn't stop the woman, whose name I caught from her tag read Darcy, from saying, "Long time no see, Rex."

Rex blurted out a quick, "Hey."

I waited for him to say more, even quickly glancing at Darcy, but she gave a nod and started filling up the car. Silence drifted in, far more deafening than the roar from passing cars or the honk from two cars nearly colliding in the gas station parking lot. The temptation to peek over at Rex became painful. She appeared around our age, and she didn't smell like she associated with any other werewolves.

"All done," Darcy said. "How would you like to pay?"

"I'll go inside," I replied. "I'd like to buy some stuff."

I followed Darcy into the deliciously cool mart as another attendant hurried out to fill up a customer's gas. One of the things I loved about Jersey was how I didn't have to get my own gas like in New York or Massachusetts. I could go on about my business whether it rained or shined.

After I opened the drinks refrigerator door, I took some extra time to cool off, then I grabbed two bottles of water before I headed to the register. I had to wait a bit while Darcy rung up another customer.

Once she got to me and took my cash, I couldn't resist asking, "How do you know Rex? Are you from this area?"

Her slow smile spoke volumes. "I haven't seen him for a long time, but we went to college together."

"So you went to Ocean City College, too? I know him from high school," I explained.

"You two smell similar. South Toms River pack, right?" She glanced out the window to my car. Rex had the window down and he stared off toward the Parkway, revealing the hard lines of his profile.

"It's good to see him," she added. "He hasn't been around in a long time."

"That's too bad. He's been south of here the whole time."

"No surprise there," she said softly. "Especially after what he did to the baseball team's captain back in college."

Now that got my attention, but I didn't want to pry. Rex might be able to hear us.

There weren't any customers behind me so Darcy kept speaking. "Don't get me wrong. Rex was a really good guy, but only when other people didn't tell him what to do. After he acted all high and mighty, things went sour with the team." She made a face as if she tasted something bad. "I'm surprised he showed his sorry face around here."

I tried to think of something positive to say about Rex—maybe even stretching the truth—but I couldn't think of anything, so I thanked her and left.

With a tank full of gas, we headed to Silverton. We passed through a quiet neighborhood, with many of the homes having motorboats and pontoons parked in the driveways.

At the end of the main drag, we finally reached the business district off the Silver Bay marina.

Through magic, I spotted the enchanted sign for the *Cornish Craftsman Company*. The shopfront had an Old West theme, even with ties for horses in the front and a water trough.

Two humans, carrying their bags of purchases left as Rex and I headed inside. Like any other countryside hardware store, the tommyknocker's mystical shop had merchandise for humans on the main floor. There were all sorts of bins with feed for chickens and bookcases with manuals for back-yard rabbit care. Past the entrance, the walls were lined with tools from familiar names and brands. As to where I'd find the hammer, I suspected I wouldn't find the magical stuff next to pricey power tools.

A bit deeper into the store, I spied a magical set of stairs leading down to another floor below.

I pointed to the left. "We should go down the stairs."

"What stairs?" Rex murmured. "I don't see any."

"Just stay close. When my foot stomps, I'm going down the first set of steps."

Rex trailed after me as I headed down a set of stone steps leading to a cavernous bottom floor. Our footsteps echoed until we reached the bottom. For a shop right off the river, this was unexpected. Rex stumbled twice, but he followed my advice and kept close.

"This is…wild," Rex whispered.

While the quiet floor above was filled with human customers, the cavernous, mystical part of the store below had all sorts of creatures scurrying about. In one section, a lithe fairy examined massive drill bits. The creature hefted up the metal checking for any defects. On the opposite side of the shop, a brownie and a dwarf couple squabbled about the quality of the magical sanders versus the lathes.

"You should never use a human lathe," the dwarf grumbled. "They break down the minute you touch them."

"But they're cheaper!" the brownie griped. The creature climbed up the side of the lathe to sit on top. It was barely tall enough to reach my knee.

Another creature wearing a dark green apron materialized beside them. "You got what you paid for. The humans don't know how to make tools that last." He turned to the dwarf couple, revealing a head full of glossy black hair and a white and pepper beard. Hope that was the store owner.

"Good sir and madame, are you interested in buying anything?"

"We need more time." The dwarf fellow dismissed the brownie who continued to examine the buttons and handles. "We're buying dowry gifts for our son's upcoming nuptials."

I held in a chuckle. Nothing like a lathe and sander to top off the wedding gifts.

The tommyknocker disappeared with a quick sparkle and materialized in front of Rex and me. "May I help you, good Madame." He gave me a pensive look with eyes far too large for the tiny spectacles perched on his wide nose.

I took a deep breath before I introduced myself. This had to be handled carefully. "Are you Mr. McSteed?"

"Yes, I am. I own this establishment."

"Wonderful, I'm interested in the silver hammer you have up on the wall over there. It's quite lovely."

And quite expensive, too. From where we stood, I couldn't miss the tiny price tag which read *two thousand dollars*. No wonder Seamus wired me the money.

"Why do you want that?" Mr. McSteed asked. "It's a very powerful weapon and in the wrong hands it could be dangerous."

"Sounds like my kind of hammer," Rex said with a grin. "It's huge. How much does it weigh?"

"It's light as a feather to the right wielder." McSteed's bushy white eyebrows rose. "The wrong one will find it far too heavy...and expensive."

Rex shrugged.

I licked my lips and considered a plan of attack. Family feuds always made things awkward. And if my memory served me right, tommyknockers and Irish leprechauns were distant cousins.

"I need protection from a powerful enemy." I withdrew the goblin blade from the holder on my ankle. "Right now, I use this for protection, but I fear it won't make do for a..." I paused to reconsider but forced myself to blurt out the rest. "A goddess's hunting hound."

McSteed's lips formed a straight line. "Hmm, I see." He paced a bit. "The last owner had fought a hydra with the hammer, but he was a powerful wizard using white magic. This weapon wouldn't be compatible with your Old Magic, I'm afraid."

"So it was a wizard's weapon, like a staff?" I asked.

"Indeed. There are only three of these that the renowned wizard, Burgess of Ingress, forged when Mount Vesuvius erupted." His grand speech quieted. "The hammer has a long-storied history, but I'm afraid you wouldn't be able to use it to protect yourself. My sincere apologies, madame."

"What if I wanted it? You know, for my tool collection?" Rex asked.

"No," we both said at the same time.

I scrambled to think of another excuse. Telling him about Diana had got me nowhere. I considered using Nick as an excuse, but I didn't have the heart to lie to such a nice fellow.

"Mr. McSteed, the truth is I need the hammer for someone else. A leprechaun named Seamus asked me to buy it from you."

Rex gave me an exasperated look.

I continued. "I honestly do need more protection from Diana's hounds, but he hired me as a stock buyer and I'm here to see if you'll sell it to me."

The tommyknocker stuffed his small, yet thick hands into his apron pockets. "Madame, the minute you walked in and glanced at the hammer, I knew." He chuckled a little. "Werewolves don't frequent this part of my store."

I nodded. Not much could be done now.

"But look, I value honesty," he said. "And you've been forthcoming about your circumstances. Few creatures can see the marks from what was around your neck."

I gasped. "You can tell?"

"Yes, madame. Those collars were crafted in the Old Country. They used tools from my kinfolk. Their handiwork leaves a mystical mark, you could say."

I brushed my fingers against my collarbone as my stomach lurched painfully. Somehow, I pushed the errant thoughts aside to focus on leaving. "At least it's gone."

"If Seamus would've been brave enough to see me," the tommyknocker said firmly, "we could've mended our differences, but he is as slimy as they come."

"Pretty much," I agreed.

"You must've fallen for one of his schemes." His wizened features reflected sympathy. "For that, I wish you well."

It was time to go.

"How would you like to pay for the hammer?" he asked brightly as if nothing had happened. "Cash or credit?"

My mouth fumbled the words at first. "You'll sell it to me?"

"I have to. You've been truthful but if I know Seamus, you have a steep price to pay if you don't bring the hammer."

"I do, and I'm grateful," I admitted. I fished my card out of my wallet.

Minutes later, two grand leapt out of my bank account

into the tommyknocker's. McSteed teleported over to the far wall and fetched the hammer. He jumped back over to us.

"Here you go," he said.

Before I could grab my purchase, Rex reached out for it. He grasped the handle with a triumphant grin—only to grunt as the hammer fell with a heavy thud to the rock floor.

"Told ya, good sir." McSteed grasped the handle and easily passed it to me. "'Tis a picky tool like all the powerful ones."

Gingerly, I grasped the handle. In my hand, the smooth metal tingled. As McSteed had said, the hammer weighed nothing.

"How come she can hold it?" Rex grumbled.

"Are you sure you want the answer, *good* sir?" McSteed's emphasis on the word "good" made me laugh.

"Naw, Nat. Let's go. Hey, wait." He scanned the immediate area. "Have you seen anything weird around here?"

"Weird like what?" McSteed asked. He glanced around his shop.

"*Rex,*" I said between clenched teeth. We got what we needed and here he was ready to poke his snout where it didn't belong. We already had enough trouble with the other shops in South Toms River.

"It's nothing." He headed for the steps.

We quickly left the store with me holding a big ass hammer and Rex sulking down the aisle. As I put the hammer in my trunk, I breathed a sigh a of relief, but the moment passed too quickly. The tommyknocker's reminder of the collar and the goddess's power couldn't be forgotten so easily. The goblin blade had gotten me out of many life-threatening situations, but even I knew it had its limits. I might have to do the one thing I promised I'd never use again: Old Magic.

To push me back on course, I got in the car. My vibrating

phone jolted me out of the moment. It was Wilhelm of all people.

Please be good news, I prayed.

"Is everything okay?" I asked.

"Not really," he said softly. "Bill told me the local shop-keepers are holding a meeting a week from now."

"It's about the curse, right?"

"I'm sure of it. Have you ever been to one?"

Between the curse and the goddess, I had far too many problems stacking up around me. "Never, and I'm quite sure if they're meeting, the situation is more dire than we thought."

CHAPTER FOURTEEN

After that lovely phone call with Wilhelm, the sunshine and clear skies did nothing to brighten my mood. Even the packages waiting on my doorstep—like the bright red blender and Happier Holidays case—were a reminder of my faults instead of the positive things I had going for myself.

To ensure my mood didn't drag my poor husband down with it, I headed over to my parents' house. The mid-summer sun had yet to set, but the sounds of laughter and the TV floated out of the Colonial's open windows. Mom had already cooked dinner, but nobody would balk if I warmed up a plate.

When I walked in, I found Dad on his recliner. The familiar sight made me grin. Dad's socked feet were propped up, his smile carefree. Whenever I came home late from hanging out with friends, he used to wait for me like that.

"Hey, Dad." I patted his arm.

"Is Thorn with you?" he asked.

"Not this time. I wanted to see everyone by myself."

"Get something to eat, then come sit with me." He

gestured to the TV with his remote. "The good part is coming soon."

"Sure thing." I was already at ease. My parents' place was magical like that.

Grandma and Mom quietly chatted in the kitchen, so I headed that way. My nose told me Mom had made stuffed peppers and rice. Every now and then, she mixed things up and skipped the meat. Instead of finding them enjoying a conversation over dessert, the two women examined a bunch of stuff on the table.

I glanced over Mom's shoulder. "What are you doing?"

A small stack of papers were filled with Grandma's chicken scratch notes in Russian, while other piles of maps and library books were scattered from one corner to another. Some notes were faded as if Grandma had collected them for a long time.

"Just some research." Mom used her backside to bump me out of the way.

"Research on what?" I picked up an old Maine map from the 1880s. "You have quite the haul here. What are you looking for?"

"I remembered something not too long ago," Grandma murmured. "Your mom's helping me search for a very special shop."

I laughed a bit. "I live for this kind of thing. Why not ask me?"

"You've got enough on your plate." Mom prepared some hot tea and pushed a cup into my hands. "Take your grandma into the living room. Your father is watching her favorite show."

"Mom, every show is her favorite." I held the steaming cup for a bit and stared her down with suspicion. What were those two doing? "Why does Grandma need to find that shop?"

"Go, go." Mom twisted my shoulders around, gave me a hard peck on the cheek, and sent me on my way.

Not long after, I joined my *babushka* on the couch as she watched recordings of old Russian TV game shows with Dad. Two hours of hearing my grandma guffaw at the contestants' antics did my heart good. And who wouldn't feel better seeing some dude rub melted butter over their hairy belly for fifteen thousand rubles?

Grandma Lasovskaya patted my hand. "You're smiling now. That's good."

Briefly, I rested my head against her shoulder. She reached up with her left hand and stroked my cheek. Her murmurings, which blossomed in my mind to a clear picture, rocked me while my eyes drifted shut.

"Are you going to tell me why you're looking for that shop?" I asked.

"No, but I'll tell you a story you haven't heard before. About me and your *dedushka*."

I cherished every story about grandpa.

"Long ago, back in my tiny village, I lived with my parents," she whispered. "It was a simple time. Young girls like me grew up with their packs, hunting in the summers and protecting their villages during the cold winters. Many suitors knocked on our door for my hand in marriage—most of them scruffy looking fellows—and I rejected them." She made a dismissive noise. "My beloved Pyotr was a cunning one, though. He told me he'd spied me from afar when he visited my village one winter, but he was too shy to speak. He waited through the spring, and when the summer heat arrived, he brought me gifts."

A girlish giggle shook her shoulders. "He left me pretty violets next to my water bucket. When I collected eggs, I found he'd tucked hyacinths between the holes in the chicken coop. He even weaved a crown for me from the wheat harvest."

She patted my knee. "But one day, the gifts stopped coming. For days, I wondered what had happened to him. I searched and searched through the countryside, but I hadn't thought to check the village itself, or the newest tiny house near the edge. It was there I found the home Pyotr had been building all summer. He'd exhausted himself and now lay sleeping inside. Without a second thought, I nursed him back to health, bringing him food and water. As his strength returned, my heart told me that beautiful house could be my home, too. We could build a family together, filling it with love and laughter."

I smiled as she stroked my hand. I wished I could've met him. Maybe see his face as vividly as she saw him back then. Did he look like my dad?

Grandma continued. "We had difficult winters with little food and an unspeakable summer when our third child died, but we always had each other. Never forget your family. Never forget that we've stood together during the tough times."

"I won't, *babushka*."

I took her hand and kissed her precious palm.

Less than an hour later, I headed home. I almost forgot about Grandma and Mom's little project. With time, I'd figure out what they were up to. Aunt Vera probably knew and she couldn't keep a secret.

Right as I got into the car, another text message hit my phone. Between the messages from Bill and that damn leprechaun, this better be spam. My fingers flew into a rapid rage to press the DELETE button, but the name of the sender made me pause.

Hello, Natalya. This is Dr. Frank. I haven't seen you in group therapy lately. As one of my diligent patients, I know you're trying your best right now. Remember what I've taught you. Believe in yourself. Just in case you find the time, I hope to see you tomorrow afternoon to chat with friends. We're here to support you.

Like my grandma, that wizard always seemed to know when I'd scraped the bottom of an empty well. I stared at the message, unsure what to do. Maybe in the morning, like all unanswered questions, I'd figure out the answer.

The next day snuck up on me and Dr. Frank's message formed a barnacle on my side. Since we had fewer customers, I had less stock to sort or rearrange on the work floor.

By mid-day, I gave up and decided to drive to Manhattan. It was group therapy day and the dog shit had hit the wall, after all. Maybe some time with Dr. Frank and my friends would help me shake off the leprechaun's tasks.

The temptation to do a bit of shopping—just a little—added buoyancy to my mood. New York City hid far too many boutiques, street stands, and other places where I could find treasures. Those tiny little temptations needed a home.

As I parked my Nissan in a parking garage, I laughed. Hadn't I already bought enough from the shopping network? (Not really.) But then again, maybe I'd run into Mike's Magical Cart. A skewer or two of well-seasoned meat sounded divine.

Soon enough, I reached Dr. Frank's Upper West Side

office. To my surprise, I couldn't find the meeting place on the right floor. I met a confused Tyler the dwarf outside of a dentist's office.

"Hey, Nat." He gave me a wave, looking his dapper self. He wore a white T-shirt and jeans, the standard attire for a model going to auditions.

"Looks like Dr. Frank had to move," I said.

"Guess so." He frowned and ran his hand through his blond hair. His shirt had countless wrinkles, but all that man needed was a wind machine, a stony expression, and he'd be ready for a men's cologne commercial.

"I didn't bother checking the sign on the ground floor," I admitted.

"Me neither."

Both our phones dinged at the same time. It was a message from Dr. Frank about the new meeting location.

I snorted. "I'd bet money this is an exercise for folks like me. He waved that wand of his and swapped shops."

Tyler pressed the button for the correct floor. "I don't mind change—I'm in a fast-paced business, but I feel for you and Raj."

The elevator doors opened, and the man, or the minor Indian deity in question, appeared. He wore his usual attire of a gamer T-shirt and jeans. Beside him stood one of our other group members, Abby the Muse.

"Looks like our timing was good," Raj said with a frown, flashing his phone. "I just got his message."

"That's rather clever of him," Abby whispered. "Plot twist!" She worked a day job as a Muse to horror and thriller authors. Her last assignment in town must've ended well. Usually she appeared withdrawn.

Tyler and I got inside. Raj reached over with his white glove-covered hand to press the button. Instead of using his finger, he used a handy little button presser tool that looked like a key. I made a note to ask him about it later. We both had obsessive-compulsion issues, but I'd managed to tamper down my impulses a bit.

Three elevator dings later, we reached the correct floor. The receptionist greeted us with a wink and pointed to where we needed to go.

"April Fools' Day was three months ago," Raj grumbled.

Abby giggled and I just shook my head with a grin.

Once we got inside, everything was arranged as expected: Eight seats formed a circle with the large mahogany table moved to the side. We even had fresh coffee, tea, and donuts on a small end table. Dr. Frank waited for us.

Raj said something in Hindi to Dr. Frank and wagged his finger. Maybe he chastised him.

Dr. Frank's lips tilted up in a half-smile.

I took a seat between Raj and Abby.

Tyler sat next to Dr. Frank. "Is anyone else coming?" he asked.

"Not today," Dr. Frank explained. "Nick is busy with medical school and Lilith is visiting her in-laws in Russia." He nodded to everyone, and I waited for him to do his white magic to lessen everyone's anxiety.

Soon enough, Dr. Frank's magic bathed the room. The tension in my shoulders eased and Abby's eyelids drooped. The lopsided grin on Tyler's face said it all: we all needed a pick-me-up now and then.

"It's great to see you all—in the right place. My apologies for my little trick. Last week, we talked about adapting to major changes in our lives. Raj didn't have much to contribute so I switched things up this afternoon. How are you feeling right now, Raj?"

The Indian deity folded his arms and briefly closed his eyes. "Not the best. My company has a major deadline for a big gaming company. Everyone around me is stressed and I can't make things better."

"Does your team need my help again?" Abby offered.

Raj brightened a bit. "You've helped us once before and I don't want to take advantage of you again."

"It's no biggie." Seeing her smile made everyone do the same.

"I love hearing everyone support each other," Dr. Frank said. "But that still doesn't address the underlying problem— how you process a stressful situation. What can Raj do when a looming deadline is shifted? Think about your life. We all have problems we must deal with sooner rather than later."

My problems with Rex came to mind and I bit my lip.

"It's like digging for resources," Tyler said. "For us dwarves, when we run into a problem, we have to find solutions or we get nowhere. Standing still is fruitless. Raj needs to tell his boss he needs time off."

"Very true." Dr. Frank eyed me. "Let's talk more about how we simply accept things as they are, even if those things are problematic. We don't want to change the status quo because acting on the problem might result in *discomfort*." He turned to the others and added, "But sometimes it's better for that change to happen. For you and everyone around you."

My doctor's words pierced through the years of my time with Rex, revealing the wounds I'd stuffed away. "How do you change yourself and face the discomfort?" I finally asked.

"By facing the cause head-on," Dr. Frank suggested. "Talk about your feelings with family and close friends. That initial pain may never go away, but over time things can improve."

Before I could change my mind, I told everyone about my history with Rex, and how I had to work with him now. Talking about his underhandedness and betrayals lifted my spirits. Everyone nodded with sympathy.

"I'd shove a battle axe up his ass to put him in his place,

but that won't solve the problem," Tyler said with a laugh. "Rex reminds me of the last casting call I had. The production director was there and he killed the mood from the get-go. Everyone dealt with him by staying calm and speaking up for themselves. They set boundaries and didn't accept his bullshit."

After we wrapped up our discussion, Dr. Frank gave us our assignments for next week. He stood and asked everyone to do the same. "Don't forget how hard you've worked to come here today." Conviction shined in his eyes. "You didn't have to come, but you made the positive step to look within and recognize the work to be done.

"Now, Raj. Your deadline isn't going anywhere. This problem is bigger than you can manage on your own." The wizard's head tilted in sympathy. "The humans will work themselves to nothing. This is your chance to lead. Speak up for your co-workers. Use your gifts to bring a voice to others who cannot speak for themselves."

Raj hung his head, then nodded.

Dr. Frank spoke to Abby next. "I do like the idea of you helping Raj, but I want him to speak to his employers on his own. You should be working on visiting that author you've avoided for the last twenty years."

Abby gave Dr. Frank a searing glare.

"I'm not saying speak to him," Dr. Frank added, undaunted. "You've conveniently had clients out of town every time this particular author comes to New York. You need to face him, Abigail."

For Tyler, our therapist simply asked him to attend a group matchmaking dinner with other dwarves. Tyler agreed, but his shiny smile had dimmed.

Finally, Dr. Frank turned to me and I knew what was coming. "Natalya, we've talked about how every hardship is a lesson we must repeatedly face. I want you to speak with

Rex, and during the next two encounters, you must set boundaries. I know you've spoken up for yourself in the past, but you need to do *more*."

I cringed, knowing he was right. As much as I didn't want to deal with Rex, we worked together now. More snide comments and back-handed gestures were coming and I could be ready for them or let them knock me down.

CHAPTER FIFTEEN

Two days passed without a new task from Seamus. I had less than two weeks left. I poked him and got nothing back. The temptation to run through town chasing my tail came to mind, but I put my nervous energy to use to hatch a plan: I'd improve my working relationship with Rex and feed his family at the same time. A win-win.

That morning, I told my mate about my dinner plans.

"You've had a lot on your plate lately," he said. "Are you sure you want company? My dad left not too long ago."

"We should do it before I think of an excuse."

He kissed my cheek, lingering long enough for me to sigh. "I'll call Rex and see if he can come by on Saturday with his brothers." He added another peck. "I'm proud of you."

"You can be proud of me *after* this is all over."

With *Operation Normal Damn Dinner* in place, I headed to work. Hours later, after I survived another winery tour party at The Bends, I stopped off at the Dalton family butcher shop for some burger patties. With tons of bags in hand, I arrived home with enough time to tidy up a bit. Not that the house needed it. After each shopping binge, I'd stowed away my prizes where they belonged in the kitchen or tucked away in one of my ornament bins.

After I hauled the food into the kitchen, I noticed a letter on the edge of the kitchen table. Had I missed this one from the pile, or had Thorn singled it out before he left for work? The return address read Birch Brook Farms, but based on the handwritten script, the envelope couldn't be an advertisement.

> Dearest Natalie,
>
> Pardon the confusion, I've forgotten your name already. I've settled down in Maine for the summer. These long summers days are always dreadful. Anyway, I thought I'd ask about those very, very expensive jade beads. Have you found them yet?
>
> Best Regards,
> MM

I swallowed down a snort. Mademoiselle Midnight *still* wouldn't be getting back her jade beads anytime soon. They had yet to make an appearance. I tossed the mail over into the bill pile. With my luck, I'd have another debt to pay in the future.

Since Thorn ran into overtime at the mill, I fired up the grill and tossed on the burgers and brats. We had plenty of leftover Russian side dishes, but I opened a can of baked beans just in case.

Now for the liquor. I added a couple of beers in the fridge and said a quick prayer with a snort. After learning we had a clurichaun, or a liquor-loving fairy, in our cellar, we didn't bring alcohol into the house anymore. I tapped the bottle tops, counting out six Budweisers. If one of them disappeared, I'd know the fairy had woken up again. Better to be safe than sorry.

By the time the irresistible aroma of dinner filled the backyard, our first guests arrived. Rex's brothers, Benny and Melvin, rang the doorbell. They sniffed around the porch until I let them in.

"Good evening!" I said. "Hope you're hungry." I hadn't spoken to them since the frost giant attacked my place. The guys kept to themselves, mostly mumbling and wandering from the South Toms River Park to their trailer where they played video games.

"Smells good." Melvin waved at me. His gray hoodie had to be horribly hot in the summer, but he donned it without a single line of sweat.

Benny skipped the formalities and waltzed inside. For once, he hid his curly mullet under a New Jersey Devils cap and wore a clean T-shirt with the team's bold red logo on the front. It was nice to see him cleaned up.

Not long after Rex's brothers showed up, Thorn got home.

"Looks like you got everything started." He glanced around the kitchen to see if I needed help. Benny and Melvin sat in the lawn chairs outside and stared at the deep bowl firepit I set up. The crackling fire set a relaxed mood for a sunset dinner.

"No need to help. I got it," I said proudly.

The doorbell rang. "Except the door," I added.

Thorn answered it and welcomed Rex. From the kitchen, I caught him saying, "Glad you could make it."

"Winston over at the bar tried to make me work, but I got out of it," Rex drawled. "I brought some beer."

"You didn't have to," Thorn replied. "We got some."

"Not that god-awful piss you buy. I brought the good stuff."

I smacked my lips in annoyance and kept trucking along. With our last guest's arrival, we could eat. "Everyone help yourself," I yelled. "There's plenty."

Benny scrambled up to the hot dog buns first while Melvin shuffled over to the plates and napkins. Rex made himself comfortable—in Thorn's usual spot closest to the house—and surveyed the yard like a king about to give a grand speech. Only the crickets chirped for their sovereign.

"Bring me a plate of food," Rex barked at his brothers.

Like one of Quinton's obedient zombies, the younger Chapman brothers took what they held in their hands to assemble a plate. Benny dumped his two brats on top of Melvin's baked beans and potato salad. As to be expected, Rex didn't thank them, and he got to work on his mountain of smashed-together food.

I turned on the backyard radio to the classic rock channel then jumped over to make sure the s'mores station had enough fixings. Benny had eyed the chocolate the minute he sat down. With each task, I kept my hands busy as I prepared to apply what Dr. Frank taught me.

Be like Bruce Lee, I thought. *Flow like water around an immovable rock.*

Thorn took a seat next to Rex and they chatted about the upcoming football season. I took in my mate, who tolerated his best friend over the years. No, *tolerated* wasn't the right word.

He accepted Rex just being himself.

Growing up I'd heard countless conversations between those two, but I never considered Thorn's perspective. I listened as they chatted.

"Do you think the Chargers got a shot at the playoffs again?" Thorn took a big bite of his burger.

"Not a chance. Their defensive line is trash." Out of nowhere Rex shot a glare in Melvin's direction. "I saw you drove the Impala here. You got money for gas?"

Melvin froze in the middle of a bite. He couldn't even eat in peace. Poor guy.

"I'm just so tired of taking care of them," Rex grumbled, taking a sip of his beer. "They're both grown men."

Thorn spoke up. "I know what you mean. It can be tough when you feel like you're the one doing all the work."

Rex raised an eyebrow. "Really? You think so?"

Thorn nodded. "Absolutely. I've known your brothers since they were pups. They're good men. But I can imagine it must be frustrating if they're not doing their part. But you know what? Sometimes we gotta be the bigger person and lead by example. Maybe if you start doing less for them, they'll start doing more for themselves."

Rex considered this before nodding slowly. "Yeah, I guess that makes sense."

Thorn was a pro at this.

Encouraged, I spoke up. "The store has been hosting a lot of private parties and we're adding some evening shifts, too. If Melvin and Benny are interested, we could use a hand."

Rex looked at me skeptically, but Thorn jumped in. "That's a great idea, babe."

"I like the idea, too," Melvin piped up. "Erica is still working there, isn't she?"

"You haven't got a chance, man," Rex said sourly.

I assembled the makings for a big fat s'more and handed the plate of happiness to Melvin. He drew his shaggy hair away from his eyes and grinned.

"Melvin's got a chance with anybody if he tries," Thorn said with a beer salute in Melvin's direction.

"Thanks," Melvin said with a small smile.

Damn, I'm a fool.

I'd listened, but I hadn't really observed them like I was analyzing a tennis match. Rex served shit and Thorn appropriately countered. My mate reinforced Rex's good actions, but he was also realistic about Rex's behavior while I tended to stew over it.

While I marveled at my mate, I spied a tiny set of grubby hands reaching for the stack of beers beside Rex's chair. The clurichaun snatched a brew and used his yellowed teeth to pop off the cap without a sound. Right above the creature, Rex stuffed his face and gestured wildly about the horrible summer construction in town. The fairy took a sip, made a disgusted face, then dumped the foul liquid.

My husband nodded at Rex's words, all the while placing his beer conveniently at the end of the table next to him. Like a nimble fox, the fairy disappeared around the men and grabbed the offering. We might have a drunken fairy on our hands, but at least the creature had good taste.

I abandoned cooking to sit next to Melvin near the fire. He added some marshmallows to a roast stick and the gooey food bubbled over the coals.

"That might set a world record for best s'more." I snagged a stick to do my own.

"For sure." Briefly, he stared out into the woods. "Is it true they're looking for folks at The Bends?"

"Of course. Bill has got some problems, but I know he'll get past them. He always does."

"Then could you put in a good word for me if I applied tomorrow?" Satisfied with his melted marshmallows, Melvin assembled his treat. "I know how hard Rex is working, by the way," he added, his voice barely audible. "After dad left us, we had to figure things out on our own. Benny's still having a hard time, so I need to step up." He crammed half the s'more into his mouth and caught the crumbs.

"It's hard to wake up after a nightmare," I agreed quietly.

"I do wanna step up, but it's hard. Every time I think about applying at the Dollar Mart or even the bakery, I remember I'm a high school dropout." He shrugged as if it was nothing, but I knew better. "Rex has it all. He moved out. He went to college."

I tossed him some more marshmallows. "College is overrated."

"Then why do employers want people with degrees?"

"Honestly, it depends on the job, but I believe it's a balance of experience and drive. A hungry worker with years of experience and determination is just as valuable as a college grad with an expensive degree."

"Well, I think so."

"Have you ever thought about getting your GED?" I suggested.

He nodded.

"One of the pack members teaches at the high school, too. He might have resources."

"I'll think about it."

Melvin hadn't said yes, and he might never want that kind of help, but I'd learned more about him than I'd known for years. I opened another jumbo bag of marshmallows and added wood to the fire. With pleasant company and fireflies lighting the night, I could forget my troubles and eat for hours.

CHAPTER SIXTEEN

Monday mornings should be tranquil like this one. After a quiet weekend and the cookout last Thursday, I enjoyed snuggling up to Thorn. I sighed and rested my nose against his back. We had to get up in ten minutes, but my mate snoozed away, likely dreaming of fly-fishing with me in Maine. I tried to close my eyes to get a couple more minutes of sleep, but the nagging feeling at the base of my spine was like a splinter. No matter how hard I tried to skip after Thorn into dreamland, the memory of Diana's collar steadily reached for me. Thoughts of an endless Christmas dinner party and presents galore were no match.

I gave up with a groan and shifted to get up, but Thorn's hand shot out to tug me to him.

"Ten…umm seven more minutes," he said.

"Can't sleep." I bumped my forehead against his wide shoulder.

"Then breathe with me." He wrapped my arm around his waist. "Six minutes won't hurt."

"Six minutes won't hurt," I repeated.

Instead of shallow, cleansing breaths, he stretched out each exhale.

When the alarm clock belted out a lively jazz tune, I reached over to turn it off, but he locked onto me.

"Is something wrong?" I almost laughed. What *wasn't* wrong?

"I went ahead and booked a cabin up in northern Maine."

"Thorn…it's not a good time."

"It's not for a vacation." Finality dripped from the word *vacation.* "We might need a place to go."

"We won't." I bit my lower lip until I drew blood. "I've had time to think about it and I refuse to believe a goddess would care about somebody like me."

"Nat—"

"Greek mythology is full of stories where gods like Zeus or Apollo had their little flings with shiny humans. Once something better showed up, Zeus dry-humped the next cool thing."

"We can't guarantee that."

"We can't, but we can hope for a normal life."

His grip loosened and he blew out a long sigh. "I'm not cancelling the reservation."

I got up, facing away from him so he wouldn't see my face, but I knew my scent, that of my fear, betrayed me. "We might be able to use it. Just keep it."

I escaped to the kitchen to fire up the coffeemaker.

While the machine gurgled and the oven warmed up left-over egg muffins, I stared out the back window. Nothing stirred among the pine and oak trees. No predators. Just a bunch of cheerful robins chirping away and squirrels scampering about. Even our lawn chairs and the covered grill stood at attention. Everything looked damn near perfect.

And even I knew I might be fooling myself. I turned away from my window to snag a coffee cup. The urge to arrange the already lined up glasses hit hard. Instead of giving in, I closed the door. Dr. Frank's voice filtered in through the din: *"When you're faced with anxiety, you should tap into your coping mechanisms."*

So I ignored the glasses. I even ignored the soap to wash my hands. Without another thought, I showered, then donned a comfortable blouse and pencil skirt. For the past couple of months, I'd proudly switched things up, but a day or two wearing some comfy clothes would do me some good.

Right after I arrived at work, I spotted Erica and Melvin at the registers.

"How is training coming along?" I asked.

Melvin had filled out an application on Friday, and by Sunday he'd worked at the last two evening parties.

"He's really quiet, but he comes alive when he's handling customers," Erica said. "At the last private shopping party, he handled all the sales while Millicent and I pushed the products."

"Very nice," I replied. "I haven't seen the numbers yet. Are these little parties worth it?"

Erica's face wrinkled up. "The profit margins are narrow. I'd like Millicent to run the show, but she keeps setting the cocktails on fire."

Melvin joined us on the other side. "I've tackled a twenty-four-hour shift running a whole convenience mart. Why not give me a shot? You and me for the next one?"

Erica's blonde eyebrow rose in amusement. "You want to jump into the wolf's mouth already?"

"Why not? It's nice to be needed for once and the pay here is much better than the minimum wage at the 7-11." He pushed his shaggy hair out of his face and added, "Millie said the witches give nice tips after they've had Erica's happy-bubbly concoction."

"Happy-bubbly?" I asked, afraid to know the answer.

"Just a recipe from Brenna," Erica explained. "It's got a bunch of organic stuff like CBD and vitamins. I think the earth witch put weed in it, to be honest."

I about choked on my spit. "Please tell me we're not getting spellcasters high?"

Neither of them blinked.

When I folded my arms, they busted out laughing.

"Brenna didn't put weed in the drinks," Erica said quietly. "But I've been tempted."

I shuddered, imagining witches twirling and dancing across the shopping floor, their spells flinging merchandise up and down the Parkway. Yeah, not a good idea.

"Looks like you've got everything covered." I left them behind to tackle my tasks for the day.

Hours later, after processing new stock and reading endless boring invoices, I trudged out of The Bends into the late July sunshine. And when I said sunshine, I meant dry heat, hot enough to air-fry your lungs to a crisp. I walked as fast as I could to my car. The short hike from the awnings' shelter stretched out. At the halfway mark, a familiar tingle scratched the back of my neck and coursed down my spine. The wolf within me froze and I locked my legs. My gaze darted from the vacant field behind The Bends to the wavering shadows around Ramneil. For three heartbeats I listened, but nothing stirred in the woods. Only a frayed piece of paper with the words CLOSED flapped in the wind.

For once I wished I had other shoppers to shield me. I'd blend in with them as they complained about the heat and hauled their finds home.

The shrill of a delivery truck honking jolted me out of the moment. I ran to my car, almost leaping over Erica's coupe in broad daylight.

Once I reached my car, I didn't wait. I gunned out of the parking lot, only once glancing over my shoulder.

Some of this might've been nerves from the upcoming shopkeeper meeting, but I suspected something else was at hand. I'd find out sooner rather than later.

CHAPTER SEVENTEEN

Two days later, I left the house in the evening for the shopkeeper meeting. While I donned a T-shirt and jeans, I prepared myself. Bill told me not to worry, but who wouldn't when the curse remained and the Goblin Apprenticeship Program threatened to shut him down. The way I saw it, Bill might be screwed.

The late-night moon, barely a crescent in size, lit my path to Huldrefolk Collectibles. It'd been a while since I'd visited Kramkar's shop. After spending a week there as an indentured worker, I'd needed a bit of a break before waltzing back inside.

Back when the shop first opened a month ago, the troll had placed gaudy balloons and an "Open Now!" banner right in front. The balloons were still there, now deflated and dead on the ground, but I guessed Kramkar planned to milk every cent out of his purchase. New customers showed up every day on the Garden State Parkway. Why not make them believe the store opened recently?

The front of the building's rock-filled garden had

crooked rows of red and green tulips. The flowers he'd stolen from the Sisters of Divine Grace still flourished under the relentless heat.

I hurried to join Harold, the owner of Archie's and a fellow pack member. His employee Jake trailed after us. We entered through the tall oak double doors. Once inside, we met several other business owners near the booth-filled space. Above us, starlight shone through the skylight windows above.

Kramkar still used glamours to hide the filthiness. He'd tossed spells all over to cover the dirty floors and add shine to mud-splattered glass. My skin crawled at the hideous sight so I took in the others around me.

Oswald, the spindly looking owner of Gray Folk Feathers, was the first one to give me a nod. The glamour-covered griffin leaned against the wall, his large, caved-in eyes taking in the other shop owners milling about.

A Black human woman offered me a cup of coffee. The mart's manager released an exasperated sigh.

"Long time no see, Jocelyn," I said.

The fatigue in her eyes lifted briefly. "Please tell me this madness is ending soon."

"I don't think so,"

Not far from us, Esmerelda and Johannas from the fairy bakery walked in. Bill, Wilhelm, and other supernatural shop owners spilled inside. Even Rex showed up.

"How bad is it here?" I asked Jocelyn.

"A shitshow. Booths are rejecting merchandise. And I kid you not, the curtain to the backroom keeps swallowing people and spitting them out."

My head twisted her way in surprise.

"Don't ask," she mumbled. "We still haven't found the DHL delivery driver."

The curtain loomed on the other side of the shopping

floor, fluttering from a non-existent wind. Better keep an eye on it.

"How are things at The Bends?" she asked.

"Beyond bad." I told her about August's murder and the warning from the Goblin Apprenticeship Program.

Jocelyn made a pained expression.

"My thoughts *exactly*," I replied.

Soon enough, folks filled the area in front of the registers, but no one spoke up until a white-blond teenager got on top of the counter. It was Kramkar. When I'd worked here, he'd stalked around like a teen kicked off the computer for gaming too long. Couldn't he have aged himself up a bit?

"Thanks for coming, everyone." Kramkar scanned the faces in the crowd, his gaze briefly locking with Bill's. My boss pushed his glasses up his nose with his middle finger.

Kramkar continued. "I'm not gonna go into why we're here. We know what's up. A goblin curse has poisoned our shops, and we need to handle the problem now rather than later. As a group, our livelihoods are at stake. Maybe our lives, too."

Bill rolled his eyes.

"Since we're all here," the troll added, "maybe Bill can shed some light on the situation."

"You know I didn't cause this," Bill said calmly.

"As if you'd admit it," Kramkar scoffed. "Everyone knows you bought Ramneil. Seems like the perfect time for The Bend of the River to grow while everyone else—"

"Enough!" Bill took a step forward as Wilhelm cowered. "Someone else is the culprit. We should find and kill them."

The Bashful Brownie Bakery chef Johannes spoke up. "And yet the curse started at your shop. For all we know, Kramkar could be right. You did this to get rid of everyone else."

"As much as I'd like *all* the profits," Bill grated out, "my customers are happiest when they can shop and eat at nearby establishments. When others succeed, I reap the benefits, too." Hearing Bill admit this sounded practical yet strange from his money-grubbing lips.

Once Bill finished his statement, I decided to step in to speak. "It's true. Bill has gone above and beyond to help. We've checked every nearby store for clues, but we haven't found anything concrete. We suspect the curse came from one of our wholesalers. It either originated from some suspicious boxes or a yatsukahagi up in Connecticut. According to the spider, he bought the goods from an overseas company called Brown Nose Associates."

Kramkar's eyebrows knitted together. "That name sounds familiar." He glanced at Jocelyn. "Can you look up that company? See if we bought or sold anything to them?"

"Sure thing." Jocelyn approached the back office curtain, then poked it with a broomstick. Satisfied the sentient cloth wouldn't eat her, she hurried into the office.

"If this becomes a bigger problem, I want to know who'll compensate me for lost customers," Johannes said bitterly.

"I don't know. Who knows what will happen next?" Kramkar drawled. "We may lose any momentum from She Who Always Walks the Path."

"How did this contagion spread?" Oswald asked. "Do we know if someone visited all the shops that became cursed?"

All eyes turned to me. My hands shot up in my defense. "I do get around, but so do a bunch of other folks around here. The culprit could be anyone. Hell, a wind witch named Mrs. Weiss frequents *every* one of your businesses. Are we gonna roll up on an old lady with pitchforks?"

I placed my hands on my hips. "If the lamps caused this, then someone could've bought the lamp from The Bends. Then for the rest of their shopping trip, they could've stopped at the other magical marts."

I'd hoped what I said made sense, but the shop owners began squabbling, and many of them pointed in my direction. Yes, I had a habit of shopping. And I'd shopped more than I should have lately, but I hadn't visited every single store until Rex and I investigated the infection. Was it possible that either Rex or myself had unknowingly spread the curse? I didn't want to think that, but it was possible. The very thought made my stomach sink.

Jocelyn returned with a piece of paper and a stony expression on her face. "It says here that Brown Nose Associates is another name for Browning Shipments. It's based out of Germany." Kramkar read off the address, and each word sparked a memory deep in my brain. *I'd seen that address before.*

"Is the VAT number for that business DE867530999?" I asked carefully.

"How did you know that?" Kramkar and Bill asked at the same time.

"I wanna know how you memorized it," Jocelyn asked.

I shrugged. "The first couple of digits sounds like that song from the eighties. My uncle Boris sang it all the time when I was a kid. It's the one about some woman named Jenny." I sang the chorus and everyone nodded.

"Oh, wow you're good," Jocelyn remarked.

"It's amazing how I remember the useless stuff," I admitted.

"So where did you see that number?" Bill asked, a bit irritated.

"Wilhelm bought a couple products from them," I explained. "He said you told him to get some cheap stuff from there."

Bill said, "I *didn't* order him to do that."

We both turned to look at Wilhelm, but he was long gone.

~

The curse Bill uttered bounced off every corner of the shopping floor. Even the sentient curtain fluttered in fear. The nose-piercing scent of red pepper floated off him and circled those around him.

I stifled a sneeze and backed away.

"How the mighty have fallen." Kramkar clapped slowly.

"Go fuck off and find a penny arcade while you're at it." Bill tossed a coin his way.

Kramkar's triumphant face fell briefly before he grinned again. "Wilhelm isn't here to admit his wrong-doings—"

"Alleged," I called out. Even I had a feeling Wilhelm was behind this, but we needed proof. And I suspected we'd missed the evidence all along. I sighed, recalling how I'd carried the boxes into The Bends, but I needed some from the back. I bet a box of hoarded cheer that Wilhelm had poisoned the boxes I put the lamps inside.

The curse had been there from the beginning.

"Sure. The way I see it," Kramkar said as he gestured toward everyone for emphasis, "the kid is behind all this, and since Bill brought him into our midst, he's just as guilty."

Esmeralda glanced away. Her uncle's scowl deepened. From behind Oswald's glamour, I caught the griffin's feathers ruffled in disgust.

The troll edged closer to Bill. "Since the goblin needs to go fetch his employee, I say we call a vote. I call for Bill's banishment from South Toms River. Is there any discussion before we vote?"

"My people are a slippery lot," Bill said with a knife's edge to his voice. "But having your so-called vote doesn't make the problem go away. Be careful. You're starting a war."

Kramkar removed his cap to reveal greasy blond strands.

"I've been waiting for you to slip up. Your greed will be the end of you sooner or later."

"I'd like for us to consider a different vote," I said. "Yes, Bill hired Wilhelm, which means he is responsible for his employee. But if Bill finds him and ends the curse, can we consider this matter handled?"

The troll interjected with, "I say no."

Harold, the owner of Archie's, finally jumped in. "My business hasn't been affected at all, but I get why everyone's pissed. Bill's not at fault here and I agree with Natalya. Give him a week to find Wilhelm and fix things. If he doesn't, he goes."

Others nodded in agreement. Only Kramkar was in opposition and the troll mart owner stared down his adversary until he finally spoke. "The meeting is adjourned," he grated out. "For now." With that, he jumped off the counter and vanished in a puff of dust.

Bill snorted. "Always gotta be flashy and shit. He could've walked out of here like everyone else." He turned to me. "Let's go."

We filed out with everyone else. On the way out, I waved at Jocelyn.

"Keep me updated if you find him," she said. "He doesn't have much of a head start."

I grimaced, considering how difficult it had been to hunt down Bill. Where the hell would a goblin on the run go? Maybe the Goblin Apprenticeship Program offices? Ehh, Wilhelm wasn't that stupid.

Once outside, I hurried after Bill. "You want a ride over to The Bends? We should check there first."

"I'll take one," Rex said. "You coming, Bill?"

Our boss faced The Bends and defiantly stood on the flowers planted in front of the shop. Guess he'd do anything to get under Kramkar's skin.

Suddenly, Bill let out a loud guffaw.

"Is something wrong?" I asked him.

Rex's head tilted and his eyes formed slits. "That's weird. The Bends smells different. You catch that?"

The wind shifted again and the night breeze carried The Bends' scent across the Parkway. Normally, the store smelled like wood varnish and the fruity air freshener Erica left in the employee bathroom, but now it had a pungent, vinegary odor, like apples left to rot in the sun.

Bill laughed again. "Clever little bastard."

"What happened?" I asked. A quick scan over the building revealed nothing amiss.

"He just locked me out of my own place," Bill replied.

"What do you mean by *locked out*?" Fear stabbed the base of my spine. "I thought you controlled everything down to the nails?"

My employer's deadpan face confirmed my fears.

"Bill…" I stretched out his name to get his attention. "Your employees are hosting a party in there."

"Melvin is in there." Rex shifted to bolt, but I grabbed his arm.

"You can't barge in. Have you seen that place defend itself?" When the Basilisk King attacked The Bends a month ago, The Bends flipped and flopped about with floorboards and siding tossing intruders away.

Rex fished out his phone. "I'll tell him to get out of there."

"They aren't coming out any time soon." Bill scratched the back of his short blond hair. "If I was Wilhelm, I'd burn it all down."

Rex turned to Bill, ready to tear his throat out, but I stepped in the way. "We need him. Stand down."

Rex's fists flexed three times before he jerked out of my grip. "If anything happens to my brother—"

"I won't stand in your way," I bit out. "You're free to get in line behind everyone else who wants to kill Bill."

CHAPTER EIGHTEEN

After I managed to convince Rex we needed our employer's help to get inside, I turned to Bill. "So how do we get them out?"

Bill smacked his lips, then his jaw twitched. "If I were him, I'd crack open the seams holding everything together, then break the store apart. While he's busy doing that, we need another Hauptschlüssel."

"A hauptsch-what? What's that word mean in English?"

"If a goblin wants to create a business—whether it's a broke down cart or even a hut under a bridge—they need a Hauptschlüssel. With it, they can cast spells to manipulate their shop."

"So Wilhelm stole yours?" Rex asked. "You let him do that?"

"Oh, no, no," Bill said. "All goblins carry theirs. He used the curse to weaken my shop and lock me out."

"Okay, then." I sucked in a couple of cleansing breaths. "Sounds like you need a new key, and all keys require a keymaker."

My boss stared at the building hard enough to bore a hole through it. His left hand began to twitch.

"Bill, are you listening?" I pressed.

No answer.

I stepped in front of him. "Damn it, Bill. Do you know where we can find help?"

"We have to go to the goblins in New York," he grumbled.

"The Goblin Apprenticeship Program?"

"Same office, different door."

"Good. That's a start." I nodded. "How much time have we got?"

"Three hours max until he blows up the building."

Did he just say *explosion*? Lock out first. Explosion second. "Can I drive us there?"

"Normally, I'd let the shop send me there, but I guess we gotta take *public* transportation." Bill said the word "public" as if he'd seen the true horrors one could find on the subway or city bus.

"A car?" I asked.

"A jump point," Bill said.

Not long after we formed a plan, we left town to reach the first jump point north of South Toms River. I left Thorn a text message: *Big problem at The Bends. Pack members and humans trapped inside. I'm safe and helping Bill find a solution. Keep people away until I return.*

After that, I turned off my phone. Thorn had a history of running after me and he had enough to worry about with The Bends takeover. I wanted him to focus on keeping everyone safe.

The trip from town to the jump point, then the Lower East Side didn't take too long. Poor Rex lost his lunch as we landed in a dark storage room in a hotel basement.

"Just breathe through it," I advised.

His face scrunched up and he wiped the perspiration from his brow.

"You ready to go?" I added.

He gave me a nod, his face pale. "People willingly do that shit?"

"It's faster than driving into town," I explained. "Nick told me there are jump points all over the world. If you ever wanna get away and see the sights—"

"Yeah, that wasn't worth it. My soul left my body for a sec there."

After he composed himself, we made our way out of the hotel to the busy Manhattan streets. The city buzzed with pedestrians, many of them dressed to enjoy the evening. Bill led the way. Ten minutes later, he came to a halt in front of a twenty-story, art deco-style building. The beautiful structure showcased the best of the golden age of architecture with intricate carvings and ornate metalwork adorning the façade. Two imposing statues of Valkyries flanked the entrance, their swords ready to bring down any proverbial enemies.

I took a step forward, but Bill didn't follow. The building glared at him, dominating the surrounding blocks, and towering over the smaller buildings nearby. Was he waiting for something or someone? I glanced around, only seeing the usual financial district shops and vendors selling everything from knockoff designer handbags to street food. Many of the pedestrians, which included glamour-covered creatures of all shapes and sizes, darted around us.

"Quit loitering," a brass sprite spat at Bill. "Either keep moving or get out of the way."

My employer finally stalked through the turning vestibule into the lobby. Instead of a grand space, the entrance hall was cramped and dingy, with a low-lying ceiling and harsh fluorescent lighting. Even the grime on the walls gave the space a deathlike pallor. As we approached the single receptionist desk and the waiting area, I sidestepped some putrid-looking stains on the scuffed floors. So disgusting.

A goblin woman briefly scowled at us from behind the desk. She barely looked up from her computer as she pointed to the waiting area.

"I want help now," Bill said crisply. "I need a duplicate key to my office in Jersey."

I slid forward. "What he means to say *nicely* is—"

The receptionist scratched a rather large wart on her nose, then rapidly typed something. "The Maker of Keys is available in twenty minutes. Pay the seat fare and wait."

"Seat fare?" Was she kidding?

Bill fished a hundred-dollar bill from his pocket and slammed it on the counter. He stalked away while Rex and I exchanged a bewildered look. For that much money, these had better be some fantastic seats with snacks *and* a massage.

I followed Bill over to rows of olive-green chairs. Based on the pattern and stitching, the fabric hadn't been replaced since the 1940s. Bill plopped down and Rex took a seat opposite him. I found a spot in the seat next to Bill. It only took an inhale and exhale for the massive lumps in the seat to drive me bonkers.

Twenty minutes felt like an eternity as other goblins arrived, paid the seating fee, and left for their destinations. Finally, a door behind the receptionist opened, and a young goblin emerged.

"Mr. Bill, please?" the youngster squeaked out.

Bill grumbled something in German and got up. Rex and I trailed after him. Here we go. The goblin led us down a seemingly endless set of corridors painted in a sickly shade of seafoam. To add to the monotony, the speakers overhead played a barely audible rendition of that annoying music you heard when you were on hold. Doors lined both sides of the hallway, each one identical to the last, with no markings or signs to indicate where they led. If our guide left us, we'd be screwed.

Finally, after what felt like hours of walking, a strange hum began to filter through the carpeted floor. The young goblin came to a stop at a cracked open doorway.

"Is this it?" Rex whispered.

The door opened wider, revealing a cramped, dimly lit room with endless shelves on the back wall. Each shelf held countless jars of old keys. A few flickering candles illuminated a space thick with the stench of motor oil. In the center, a massive key-making machine, blackened with soot and grime, belted out fumes. Its pipes and gears reached every corner of the room like a giant metal spider.

Bill strode in first, followed by Rex. I held up the rear as the machine's gears ground and whirled with a fierce intensity. After a final sharp clunk, the key machine spat out a purple key into a tiny, old goblin woman's wrinkled palm.

The Maker of Keys beckoned us to come in from behind her cluttered desk. She tossed the key into a pile on the floor. Her piercing yellow eyes formed slits as her right hand stroked the neck of a small dragon slumbering next to her desk. The creature somehow slept through all that noise.

I waited for Bill to make another demand, but when he spoke, his voice was barely above a whisper.

"Excuse me," he said politely. "I need another key for my business."

"Do you now?" Her crooked index finger drew a circle on the dragon's scaly throat. "Should we drive him away, Morad?"

The dragon continued to snore, oblivious to the keymaker's musings. "Why do you need a duplicate key?" she added.

The muscles on Bill's face tightened. "My apprentice

conned me out of it. I destroyed his family's shop, but I suspect you already knew that."

He destroyed that poor family's shop? No wonder Wilhelm was out to get Bill.

The Maker of Keys chortled. "Typical," she muttered. "Why did you hire him in the first place?"

"I guess I felt sorry for him. He hasn't accomplished much."

"I see. I can make you a key, but it'll cost you."

Bill stuffed his hand into his pockets and fished out stack after stack of what appeared to be crisp Deutsche marks. "I hear you like 'em new—"

"Ah, ah, ah," she sing-songed. "A goblin's first set of keys are free, but duplicates are another matter." Her thin lips widened to reveal tiny teeth. "You've managed to avoid me for centuries, Bill, but it appears someone finally put you in your place."

"What do you want?" Instead of answering with malice, he replied with resignation.

"You'll learn my fee in a moment, but I'd like to know what you did to your rival."

"You already know," he bit out.

"Then tell me again," she said pleasantly. "All I do is work here. Would be nice to have my memory…refreshed as they say these days."

"Do we have time for this?" Rex hissed in my ear.

"Be quiet." I flashed Rex a dark look. "Maybe you'd like to pay the fee so she can *hurry* up!" I whispered.

Next to us, Bill clenched his trembling hand. "I *always* hated those Löchrigesleder goblins. They had the nerve to open their so-called shoe shack on the other side of the town square. From sunup to sundown, they sold their stock to any barefooted fool who'd listen. They even marched right up to my odds and ends wagon and tried to win over my customers with their slimy shit." His voice rose, bouncing off the pipes. "I considered having a little chat with them, but the odds were ten against one, so I taught them a lesson. In the middle of the night, I burned down their shack. After that, they caused me no trouble."

I gasped, unable to look at Bill. After what he did, Wilhelm wouldn't set anyone at The Bends free.

"No trouble? Nine of those ten goblins died," she said simply.

"Yes, they did," was all he said.

The Maker of Keys smiled slyly. "Owning a business is a cutthroat affair. We must work to survive, but spilling blood for profit has no honor." She tapped the worn desk for emphasis. "You *could've* ignored them. You could've outsold them and drove them out. They never would've truly harmed your business, and yet you killed them. You took the *easy* way out. For that, you'll give me a precious thing: your last name."

Bill's twitching hand froze, and my stomach dropped. I'd never heard anyone refer to his last name. Even the mail at The Bends didn't refer to it.

"My last name is Möbelbauer," he said, reluctantly.

The Maker of Keys cackled. "'Tis nice to hear it out loud."

Bill said nothing, his anger evident in his stiff demeanor.

"Well then," she said. "I think it's high time you learned a little humility. Give me your left hand."

Bill held out his hand, watching as the Maker of Keys placed it on the key making machine's nearby pedestal.

"We need a special key, Morad!" She poked the sleeping dragon's head. The creature flared to life and shook its floppy ears. After a quick stretch, the dragon's long neck craned all the way to the top of the machine. Morad inhaled deeply, then blew a string of burnt-orange fire down one of the open pipes. The machine whirred to life, its gears grinding and clanging as it stamped out a new key. I tried to track the progress but couldn't figure out one end from the other. Eventually, the machine completed its task and a golden key landed in her tiny palm.

She turned the Hauptschlüssel over to Bill. After he took the key, he didn't look at me once—or thank the Maker of Keys as he stomped out.

"Thank you, m-ma'am," I stammered. "It was nice to meet you."

We escaped after him and came out the front of the building.

Rex staggered from the abrupt change from inside to outside. "Can't they warn us when they do that?"

Bill twisted sharply our way. "You heard *nothing*," he muttered. "Nothing."

Rex shrugged, but a quiver of fear tickled my stomach. He had no idea how much power knowing someone's true name had in the supernatural world. In some magical circles, a name acted as a tether. Someone with nefarious intentions could use that knowledge to cast dark spells on their victim.

My co-worker hurried after Bill, ready to break into The Bends. I hoped Rex never tried to use that knowledge for his own benefit.

CHAPTER NINETEEN

"Will the building defend itself like last time?" I asked Bill as we walked back to the jump point.

"Unfortunately," he said. "And he won't hold back like I do."

"Then we'll need a lot more help. Thorn is likely waiting for us, but I'm contacting Jocelyn, too."

The goblin picked up the pace, clearly irked with my suggestion. "Why are you asking Kramkar for help?"

"'Cause I've seen your business toss intruders like kids' toys," I bit out.

Rex and I couldn't keep up and soon Bill was far ahead of us.

"Damn, he's fast," I grated out.

"The sooner we get there, the better." Rex left me to run after Bill.

I reached an intersection, and I missed crossing in time. Of course, those two left me behind. Since I had a minute or so before I could get across, I whipped out my phone and tried to form a plan that didn't involve us getting killed.

The manager at the troll place replied first: *Kramkar refuses to help, but I told him he won't have a store if The Bends blows up so...he'll send help.*

That response didn't surprise me.

I also confirmed that Thorn held down the fort at The Bends.

Soon enough, I caught up with Bill and Rex. By the time we arrived in the parking lot at The Bends, a crowd waited for us. My gaze swept over the people willing to offer a hand at the last minute—which included everyone from the meeting. All the fairies from the bakery showed up, the werewolves from Archie's, and Oswald from Gray Feather Folks. A sizable crowd. Since it was nighttime, I expected to see Kramkar, but he wasn't here yet. From what I'd learned, his people petrified during the daytime. So why was Jocelyn here instead of him?

Thorn stepped up to me first.

"How are things?" I asked him.

"Very quiet. I tried to get inside, but all the doors and windows are locked. I couldn't break the windows either."

"As to be expected. I suspect we're going to have to break in."

"Then I'll get the pack members ready." He kissed the top of my head and joined the werewolves.

I walked over to Jocelyn. "Thanks for coming and sounding the alarm."

"Not a problem," she said. "I had a feeling you'd need a hand sooner rather than later."

"Where's your boss?" I asked her.

"He's here." She pointed to some weird boulders jutting out of the lawn in front of Ramneil's. I hadn't seen those before. "It took *a lot* of convincing to get him to help."

"I won't owe him for this, will I?" I was kidding. Just a little.

"You worry about getting in there. Just let me know when the trolls should make their move."

Thorn spoke with the werewolves from Archie's while I approached Bill, the fairies, and Oswald. I motioned for Jocelyn to join us.

"Does the roof have any defenses?" the griffin asked Bill.

"Not as many as the walls and windows," the goblin replied. "Anything can be used as a weapon. Shingles, nails, vents."

"Hey, Bill. Do you have a plan of attack you can share with everyone?" I asked him.

Bill sighed and turned to the crowd. "I guess I could say something meaningful, but you folks know I don't do that."

Harold chortled and shook his head. Somehow, Thorn kept a straight face.

Bill continued. "Don't bother with the doors. The Bends can move 'em at will. The best approach is distraction and swarming. We need to overwhelm Wilhelm so I can break in." Bill stuffed his hands into his pockets. "In closing, umm, thanks." He left it at that and walked over to the Ramneil. He opened the door and slipped inside. That goblin better be helping instead of putting his feet up.

"Any questions?" I asked to fill the awkward silence. "Stay back and stay safe, Jocelyn."

The troll mart manager nodded as the werewolves ran into the woods behind the building to shift. I hoped Rex would follow orders from Thorn and stay out of trouble.

Everyone else made their move.

In a puff of gray smoke, the griffin shifted to his natural form and took to the sky. Then he dove toward the roof, black talons extended, but as he approached, the roof shingles sprang to life, hurling themselves at the griffin like sharp, deadly projectiles. The nimble creature bobbed and weaved, but the relentless barrage drove him back.

While I withdrew my goblin blade from my ankle holder, the pack got to work. From the woods, one black werewolf and three light-colored ones came racing out to leap onto the back of the building. Rex stormed ahead of Thorn to slam into the back door. Thorn scampered up the gutters, only to be flung off. Ever the agile wolf, he rolled mid-air to bound back. Jake circled the side to approach the door under the awnings.

Armed with a fallen tree from the woods, the fairies stormed on the front door. They formed a line with Johannes belting out orders.

"Heave ho!" he barked.

The fairies rammed the door—only to have the entryway shift to another spot.

With a silver goblin knife in hand, I ran for the back of the store, my breath hitching. Suddenly, the ground rumbled beneath my feet. The boulders in front of Ramneil sunk into the ground. The rumble gradually grew stronger, approaching the back of The Bends faster and faster. Sooner or later, they'd hit the concrete foundation. I held my breath, hoping they breached it. The concrete dock cracked and groaned, as if under a great weight. I jumped out of the way. The stress on the dock reached its breaking point. The stone blocks fractured and the ground opened up like a hungry sinkhole, forming a gaping chasm that slurped down every-thing around it. With a thunderous crash, The Bends' back doors collapsed into the hole. More debris was sucked out of the building—including desks, tables, and other furniture. Seeing an opening, Thorn rushed for the door—only to have a flying moose head-butt him back out.

Guess I wasn't getting in that way.

I leaped over the hole and joined Jake. He jumped from perch to perch, unable to sink his claws into the siding. I sunk the blade in deep. The Bends' shuddered, unable to shake me off. The building went still for a moment. All at once, everyone moved. Oswald landed on the roof. Harold crashed through a window.

And the strangest sight of them all, the Ramneil *moved*. A bunch of the abandoned boards and building supplies in the back jostled, then they scrambled like sentient Lego blocks, stacking one on top of the other. Gradually, the rectangular studs and roofing material made their way from the Ramneil toward The Bends, forming an aboveground tunnel of sorts.

The wound where I'd punctured The Bends shuddered to shake me off.

"You're not getting rid of me that easily." I held firm.

Behind me, the Ramneil tunnel resembled an approaching freight train, coming faster and faster until the materials met the side of The Bends. The siding emitted a hollow groan. Cerulean sparks swirled and danced, growing brighter until I had to squeeze my eyes shut.

With a heavy thud, the tunnel merged with The Bends. A glimmering red light stepped out of the Ramneil. It was Bill. The goblin advanced through the connective structure until he reached The Bends. From there, he entered the building through a widened gap.

"Hole in the back!" I yelled.

The wolves abandoned the windows, the fairies the front door. The griffin jumped off the roof to join us. I hurried in after Bill to utter chaos on the main shop floor.

Wilhelm stood in the center, surrounded by a chaotic whirlwind of antique trinkets and furniture. The magical wind screamed as floorboards and drywall were gobbled up.

"I was hoping you'd run away, Bill," Wilhelm taunted. "Guess you'll have to watch me destroy this place from the inside out."

In the corner opposite to where I stood, Erica, Melvin, and Millicent were locked in a fierce battle against enchanted merchandise. The humans cowered behind them. Erica swung the heavy mace in wide, powerful arcs, shattering wooden chairs and bookcases. Every impact sent splinters flying.

While Melvin protected the humans with his bat, Millicent raised her palms and unleashed waves of heat. Magical capes swooped and swirled through the air at them like menacing birds of prey. One particularly aggressive cape dove in and wrapped itself around the fire witch's face. It attempted to drag her up the wall, but the fire witch singed the fabric until it released her.

They needed help. Time to kick some ass.

The goblin blade lengthened and vibrated in my hand as I advanced around Wilhelm to reach the others. I swung hard, the shimmering blade slicing through the air. I severed the grasping tendrils of enchanted rugs and deflected the sharp edges of animated picture frames. One frame darted around me to knock away the griffin. Rex tried to sprint ahead of Thorn and the pack.

"Get back, damn it!" I shifted right to dodge a spinning teapot set.

As if in response to my warning, one of the capes suddenly snaked around Rex's neck, yanking him off his feet and flinging him to the wall. He crumpled to the floor, yelping in pain.

While Erica sent a Victorian cupboard flying with a powerful strike of her mace, I deftly jumped over a pack of taxidermy animals that had come to life. They snapped and clawed at my heels. I scrambled towards the others, my sword knocking back anything in my path.

Erica and I joined forces, our weapons striking in unison to create a protective barrier around the others. Meanwhile, Thorn and the pack acted as a distraction. With a final, resolute push, we drove the enchanted furniture back, allowing the humans to sprint for Bill's opening to the outside.

In the center, Wilhelm glanced at the escaping humans. He flicked his fingers to drop drywall over the opening. The furniture and floorboards flying through the air caught fire. Bright lights from the flames lit the chaotic sales floor.

"Enough!" Bill roared. The crimson light bathing his body contracted, then exploded into an inferno. The broken wall sections shifted out of the way. The maelstrom around Wilhelm twitched mid-air—only to rotate to the left instead of the right. No longer caught in Wilhelm's spell, debris rained down from above toward the apprentice.

With Wilhelm occupied, I turned my attention to Rex. Erica and I moved cautiously, keeping a watchful eye on the still-animated objects. I stood my ground with the pack while Melvin hoisted Rex onto Thorn's back. They formed a line and escaped the store.

Now only Erica and I remained.

She stood beside me, but I motioned for her to go.

"You're gonna stay?" Erica asked. "Are you nuts?"

"Wilhelm still might blow up The Bends," I bit out. "Get the others to safety."

Erica slipped out the opening as Bill thrust his hands forward. The flaming floorboards were extinguished as they snapped back on the floor. The wayward registers floated over to a corner.

Wilhelm smirked and glanced at the glass displays. The metal and wooden fixtures jerked then coiled around Bill like a python.

Trapped within the warped materials, Bill groaned. I scrambled to assist, but the floor under my feet shifted to fling me across the room. As I sailed through the air, I dropped the goblin sword. The ground came at me too fast. I landed on the taxidermy animals I'd escaped earlier. My elbow absorbed the blow and broke with an audible *crunch.* Ouch. A herd of deer stormed at me. Right behind them, a polar bear loomed on all fours. It rose high above me and bared its teeth. Then it hit me again. Suddenly, the world started spinning as it sent me sprawling. When I came to a stop, I glanced around in a panic. My vision swam in and out.

Wake up, Nat. You need to defend yourself.

Where the hell was my goblin blade?

A stuffed moose head mounted on a nearby wall twitched. The moose head sprang to life, its eyes glowing with an unnatural light. It charged towards me with antlers lowered and knocked over the deer, then it raced to the glass encasing Bill. The moose head shoved its antlers between the twisted metal, then twisted and pulled to set my boss free. Bill scrambled to his feet to attack again. The goblin adversaries circled one another, hurling objects back and forth. Tables, chairs, and chandeliers soared through the air, leaving devastation in their wake. Rope from a Victorian curtain set materialized in Bill's hands. With a flick of his wrist, Bill sent the rope hurtling towards Wilhelm. It wrapped around the apprentice, binding his arms and legs.

Meanwhile, I had my own problems. I staggered to stand. The polar bear advanced again. I picked up the pace and bolted for the exit, but the deer herd blocked my path. Two stuffed ostriches flapped their wings until they drove me to a corner. There was nowhere for me to go. The polar bear closed in. Raised its paw high. Before it's massive paw hit my head, the animal froze, then fell over with a thud. I stared at the sharp claws before unnatural laughter bubbled up my throat. Thankfully, death by taxidermy bear wasn't on my bingo card today.

My elbow and side continued to ache as I scrambled out

of the mass of stilled taxidermy animals. I found Bill next to a trussed-up Wilhelm.

Bill gestured toward an empty cedar chest. The box bounced over and gobbled up Wilhelm before the hatch slammed shut.

"You'll stay in there until you lift the curse on all the magical shops," my boss demanded, his voice firm and unwavering.

Silence was his answer.

"Okay, then." Bill twirled his fingers. The chest shook like a cocktail shaker. Wilhelm screeched.

"You ready now?" Bill asked.

"You killed my family," a voice croaked from inside the box. "I want justice."

Bill stiffened.

"How is this justice?" I stammered. "Do you deserve that after you killed August?"

"He was in the wrong place at the wrong time," was all Wilhelm said.

Wow, these two deserved each other.

"Say something, Bill." I took a step forward.

"You caught a bad break, kid," he said. "Too bad you gotta die today, but you know our ways. We live and die until our shops close for good."

"That's not an apology, Bill." I spotted my goblin blade off to the side and grabbed it. I might have to settle things in a not-so-nice manner.

"It's the best he'll get." Bill surveyed the war-torn store. "Stay out of this, Natalya," he warned.

"No, you can't kill him." I limped over until I stood between Bill and the chest. "You wronged him. He struck back. Make amends and send him off to whatever jail you goblins have."

At first, Bill stood there, defiant. The seconds ticked by until he grunted, "Sorry."

From within the chest, Wilhelm muttered an incantation, and the oppressive energy weighing down the store dissipated.

With the curse removed, Bill gestured toward the chest and the hatch opened. Before Wilhelm could jump out, a crack in the floor widened to reveal the lobby to the goblin headquarters in Manhattan. The chest turned onto its side and dumped the apprentice onto one of the seats in the waiting area.

"Taking out the trash for Mr. Hässlicheschuhe," Bill called down to the receptionist.

"Seating fee, please," she called out with her hand extended.

"Send me a bill." My employer laughed and sealed the floor shut.

I sank to the floor, knowing Bill would walk away from this without learning a damn thing.

CHAPTER TWENTY

God help me, last night was a nightmare. I'd like to say I woke up the next morning feeling relieved and chipper, but I accidentally bumped my broken elbow against my headboard. Around three in the morning I pulled a ninja move to turn over in my sleep and I hit the swollen spot square in the middle. Instead of crying out like normal people, I laughed maniacally until Thorn checked on me.

"You okay?" he asked.

"No, it hurts to be alive."

That got a laugh out of him, too.

Rapid werewolf healing was a benefit and all, but depending on the injury, like a moving joint, my body needed more time to stitch me back together.

"Want some pain meds?" he asked.

"Got a sledgehammer instead? You can take me out of my misery."

"I told you to put your arm in a sling, but you're too stubborn."

I muttered a couple of curse twords and gingerly slipped

my arm into a sling. After that, I couldn't sleep. For hours, I lay there, wondering what state I'd find The Bends in over the next couple of days, wondering if that lightning bird had spit out a feather yet, and more importantly, when was that leprechaun gonna send me the last job?

Watching some TV in the living room came to mind, but I'd fallen down that blackhole too often.

I got up and headed out to the living room. Instead of crashing on the La-Z-Boy, I left the house and stood on the edge of the back concrete patio. This early in the morning, cooler air prevailed and a pleasant breeze tugged at the elm and oak trees. Nothing stirred in the woods and the anxiety nipping at my senses retreated. I returned to the house. Sooner or later, my troubles would come back, but I had work to do, and work gave me purpose when I needed it.

Before I escaped the house, I carefully showered and dressed. Time to check on Rex and his family. They lived on the northwest side of town in a trailer park across the street from a baseball field and pizzeria. Most of the homes on the small lot were older with weathered siding or gravel drive-ways with weeds defiantly poking out. I drove past two quiet trailers before I reached Rex's home.

Other than his shiny truck in the driveway, folks couldn't miss the overgrown lawn or rusted folding chairs. Nobody had bothered to clean up the beer cans and overflowing ashtrays on the porch either. I sighed. No wonder Rex wanted to live on his own. Who'd want to come home to this every day?

I grabbed the bag of goodies from the fairies at the bakery and headed up to the door. After two knocks, Melvin opened up. A sour and acidic scent wafted out.

Using my good arm, I presented my offering. "I brought some breakfast. Thought I'd check on Rex." I tried to sound cheerful.

"Sure," Melvin mumbled.

The wooden door groaned in protest as he let me in. I entered, preparing myself for what I'd face, but I still inwardly cringed from the filthy clothes strewn all over the living room. Off to the side, the eat-in kitchen had counters riddled with takeout containers and a sink full of crusty dishes. Flies reigned through the house, their buzzing about as loud as the window fan.

"You hungry?" I asked Melvin.

"Yeah." He glanced at my arm. "You didn't have to come."

"I'll be fine. Doesn't hurt unless I move."

That got a laugh out of him as he accepted the sack and dug into the pastries.

"Is Rex in the back?" I asked.

"Yeah. He hasn't woken up yet."

"I won't wake him up." I ventured deeper into the trailer past the bathroom—I'm not gonna look in there—and the bedroom Melvin and Benny shared. Rex's bedroom was at the end of the hall. His partially opened door, which I discovered was broken, revealed a room draped in shadows. A shirtless Rex was curled up on the queen-size bed. He labored with each breath.

I considered speaking to him, but I imagined he wouldn't have much to say after taking a hit hard enough to scramble his insides.

"Rest up, Rex," I whispered.

When I returned to the living room, Melvin sat on the couch enjoying a tiger tail donut. He even wrapped up his food in a paper towel to catch the sugary flakes.

"He looks pretty bad," I admitted. "Make sure he doesn't hurt himself."

"Will do. Quick question. Is The Bends closed for good? I liked working there."

"Oh, no. Bill would sell out of that wreckage if he could.

He just needs time to clean up. Where's Benny?" I didn't see anyone in the other bedroom.

"He's over at a friend's house." Melvin shrugged, clearly disappointed.

"Okay, I'm heading out." I grabbed the doorknob, fighting the need to retreat from the mess, yet knowing I couldn't walk away without doing something.

Once outside, I made it halfway to my car before I dialed a number I knew would start an avalanche of care in motion: I called my mom.

Three hours later, I returned at lunchtime and couldn't help grinning until my face hurt. Five cars lined the street and folks swarmed the trailer. The Stravinskys were hard at work. My sweaty Uncle Boris draped a towel over his head as he finished up mowing the lawn. All around him, the Stravinsky kids raced up and down the street, their laughter adding levity to the quiet neighborhood. My brother and his wife attacked the front porch. Little Sveta perched on one of the cleaned-up seats and reached up for me when I walked up to them.

"My *printsessa*, have you been a good girl?" I rained kisses on her soft cheeks.

"No," her mother and father said at the same time.

I laughed. "They don't spoil you enough. You need to spend time with your *tetya*."

I picked up my nine-month-old niece with my good arm and she rested her head against my shoulder, all innocence and sticky fingers.

This time when I entered the house, the coolness hit first. Somebody had fixed the air conditioner, too.

Aunt Vera and Melvin sat on the couch folding up piles and piles of clean clothes.

"Hey, everyone," I called out.

Melvin actually smiled. "You're back already?"

"I could smell Mom's food from my house," I replied.

Mom never resisted baking and broiling for a good cause. In the time I'd been gone, someone had chiseled the food off the dishes and scrubbed down the counters. Now a pot of hearty beef stew bubbled on the pristine stove. I wouldn't be surprised if the fridge had been cleaned out and some food from Dalton meats filled the shelves.

"Why are you carrying Svetlana? You're hurt," Mom said from the kitchen. "Give my grandbaby to me."

At least Mom had a good excuse this time for her grandma thievery. I handed the child over.

"Do you need any help?" I asked.

She made a dismissive *cluck-cluck*. "You'd slow us down. Your dad just left after fixing the furnace." She mentioned upcoming visits from the pack healer and a pack member who was a plumber. "Once we got the kitchen in order, we were fine. Thank goodness, I had cleaning supplies from our spring cleaning at the church."

"Thanks, Mom."

She made a face. "You don't need to thank us. We take care of our own."

Aunt Vera nodded sagely from the living room. "You need to speak up, Melvin," she said to him. "You need clean clothes to work and food to eat. When Benny comes home, I have some things to say to him, too."

His grin spread wider and I knew he'd be all right. "Yes, ma'am."

~

After two long days of cleanup back at The Bends, I managed to find some spare time to return to the lightning bird's shop. With four days, and no message for the fifth request yet, I hoped that damn bird had a feather to pluck off for the leprechaun.

Right before the Saturday opening hours, I pulled up to the Electric Wing Lighting Co. Once I stood in front of the quaint lighting shop, its windows filled with an array of gleaming lanterns and chandeliers, I shivered, but not from the humidity. The sun had just risen, casting a golden glow on the rooftops that lined the sleepy cobblestone street. The small businesses were eerily quiet.

My heart began to race, and I couldn't shake my unease. I glanced down at the goblin blade strapped to my ankle, its presence a comforting reminder. As my fingers grazed the weapon, it seemed to hum with warmth and energy. I knew I had to be on guard, but the source of my apprehension remained frustratingly elusive.

I walked past the closed lighting shop to see if anything was amiss. My gaze swept across the street, taking in the slumbering businesses. To my left, a charming flower shop stood sentinel, its windows adorned with lush bouquets and vibrant blossoms. The shop's door was flanked by two tall pots overflowing with flowers, their colors muted in the early morning light. The air was thick with the heady scent of roses and jasmine, which mingled with the earthy aroma of damp soil.

Adjacent to the flower shop was a comic bookstore, its plate glass window filled with the colorful faces of super-heroes and fantastical creatures. The store's façade was a riot of color, with posters and signs announcing the latest releases and upcoming events. I couldn't help but smile as I thought of the joy that the comics brought to young and old alike, providing a brief escape from reality. I wished I could hold on to that feeling, too.

A vacant farmer's market occupied the corner, its usually bustling stalls and tables now empty and shrouded in shadow. The skeletal frames of the stands loomed like silent ghosts, waiting patiently for the vendors who would soon arrive with fresh fruits, vegetables, and other local goods.

Just a bunch of stores. And yet, the normalcy of these places felt like a shroud covering something ominous underneath it.

A flock of pigeons pecked at a pile of spilled birdseed near the farmer's market, their soft brown feathers gleaming in the weak sunlight. They cast nervous glances around them as if sensing the eerie stillness.

Suddenly, something in the distance caught their attention. In a flurry of wings and prolonged coos, the pigeons took to the air, their sudden departure casting a shadow over the street. My heart raced in my chest, my unease growing stronger as the birds disappeared from sight. What had spooked them? And was it connected to the strange feeling that had been haunting me all morning?

I made my way to the narrow alley that ran alongside the lighting shop. It stretched into the shadows, eventually heading into a nearby parking garage. The structure was dimly lit, several of its lights blown out. As I strained my eyes to peer into the blackness, suddenly, two minuscule red eyes trained in my direction. Determined to confront the unknown, I took a few cautious steps toward the crimson stare. But just as I drew closer, a car emerged from the garage, its headlights blinding me. Blinking away the glare, I glanced into the garage again and found nothing. I shook my head and laughed. At this point, my frayed nerves were playing tricks on me. The recent weeks had taken their toll, and I desperately needed some rest.

The sound of a lock clicking brought me back to the present, and I turned my attention to the lighting shop's door.

I stepped into the shop, the tinkling of the doorbell

announcing my arrival. The interior was cool, a far more inviting space than outside. The glow from the chandeliers cast intricate patterns on the walls and floor.

Umbane greeted me with a warm smile. "Good morning, Natalya!"

"Morning," I replied, returning the gesture. "It's been quite a morning already."

The lightning bird raised an eyebrow, his interest piqued. "Oh? Do tell."

I hesitated for a moment, considering whether to share my concerns. But as he turned on more lights in the shop, creating a cozy, comforting atmosphere, I decided to open up. "Well, I've had this unsettling feeling since I woke up, like I'm being watched or followed. I thought I saw something in the nearby parking garage, but it turned out to be nothing."

He paused in the middle of adding money in the register, his expression a mixture of concern and curiosity. "That does sound strange, but sometimes our minds play tricks on us when we're stressed or tired. You've been through a lot lately."

"I know." I sucked in a cleansing breath. "But it felt so real."

"Well, trust your instincts," he advised. "But don't let fear control you."

"True words," I replied.

After a brief silence, he asked, "You're here for a feather, right?"

My mood brightened as I remembered my purpose for the visit.

He chuckled. "I knew you'd be back soon. Let me go get it for you."

I couldn't stop grinning as the lightning bird left through the rear doorway and returned to place his beautiful feather in my palm. The feather was heavier than it appeared. From the tip down to the end of the hollow shaft, the plumage pulsated with vibrant golden hues. "This is breathtaking, Umbane."

I turned it carefully to catch the morning light. "If you're ever low on cash, you should reach out to the proprietor at Gray Folk Feathers in South Toms River."

"I'll have to remember that. Oh, and more one thing," he added. "Did you ever get rid of that curse you told me about?"

I gave him the grisly details on how the other shop-keepers broke into Bill's place and lifted the curse.

"That's a relief," he replied. "I don't get a lot of customers and I don't want to frighten the ones who do show up."

I offered him a couple of tips. How he needed a better website, a presence on social media, and he needed to take advantage of the farmer's market across the street. "Every Saturday and Sunday, you need to be outside hawking your goods. Grab something inexpensive, like those nightlights you're selling in the back."

After my way too long speech, I bid the lightning bird goodbye. At the doorway, I checked through the glass. The street was empty, but as I darted to my car, I reminded myself I had too much to do. Letting my imagination get the best of me wasn't wise.

As I left Midland Park for home, that lingering sense of unease refused to dissipate, leaving me wondering if I had truly seen nothing out there or if a hidden danger waited to strike.

CHAPTER TWENTY-ONE

Four hours later, I lounged back at the cottage with an addictive thriller novel and a glass of sweet tea. With the air conditioning on full blast, I propped my feet up on the La-Z-Boy and fell into a great book. There was nothing better than some sweet tea, explosions, and some sass. Over the last couple of months, I haven't had much time to sit in the house—especially with Farley blasting the TV at full volume. Now I could dive into my neglected to-be-read pile and clear some space for even more books.

Right as I got to a really good part, my phone vibrated on the nearby end table. I read the message on the screen and sighed.

> Sorry about the wait, lass. One of my ladies got arrested during her dinner date and I had to have a little chit-chat with the police. I need you to go to the Yule Cat in Central Park. At dusk, search for the cat's trailer around Bank Rock Bay. Once you find the finicky lady, buy five T-shirts from her.

There went resting.

I slipped a bookmark between the pages and got my shoes on.

"Where you going?" Thorn sat on the couch across from me watching a baseball game.

"I got the last task."

"He's cutting it close. You only have four days left." Thorn turned off the TV.

"What are you doing?"

"I'm coming with you."

I considered coming up with an excuse, but Thorn already had his shoes on and keys in hand. Guess I had company again. On the way out the door, I told him about the job.

"Have you ever seen a Yule Cat before?" he asked.

"Nope. I have a feeling I won't find it easily if Seamus or his girls haven't bought the clothes yet."

Since I was getting the last item and I would already be in New York, I grabbed the feather and silver hammer from my trunk. Then we got in Thorn's SUV. My stomach rumbled in protest. There went eating lunch at home. I'd marinated some chicken in adobo sauce for fajitas. As we pulled away from the house, I had a sinking feeling we wouldn't be back for a while.

"Can we stop at Barney's for a late lunch?" I asked him.

"Yeah, I'm hungry, too."

We arrived at the restaurant to find a huge school bus taking up most of the parking spots. Thorn dropped me off while he waited off to the side.

Barney's was filled to the brim with squirmy elementary students eating their lunch. They gabbed and shouted from their seats. I spied a free table—albeit a dirty one near the door. I considered snagging it until I watched a kid at the next table dig in his nose. He shoved his index finger up there with gusto, then plucked out and flung his bounty toward the free table.

So gross. I was gonna get our food to go.

I headed over to the register to find Aggie and another clerk taking the orders.

"Hey, Nat!" she said. "You're looking better than the last time I saw you."

"Thanks. Could I get my usual? I also need a roast beef combo for Thorn."

One plucky kindergartener chased down another behind me. The one in the lead crashed into a table. Even I cringed from the impact. Both kids started wailing. The teachers scrambled to check on them.

"Is she all right?" Aggie called out.

"She just bumped her head," one of the teachers replied. "She'll be fine."

"Gotta check these days," Aggie whispered to me. "Can't have that kid's mom rolling up in here. I thought your family dinners were crazy, but these kids are giving your cousins a run for their money."

"Yes, they are." I turned to see the nose picker attacked his other nostril now.

Aggie personally assembled my lunch order. "Are you two just eating out for lunch?"

"Naw, I gotta take care of the last task for Seamus."

"I thought you still have some time left. Why not rest and wait until Monday?"

"Oh, no, no. I have until *Wednesday* July 28th to get this done and I know Murphy's Law all too well. What can go wrong will go wrong, so I'm doing this *today*."

Aggie placed my food in a sack while I added, "Seamus said I'd have to wait until sunset to find the Yule Cat's cart, but I plan on hanging out in the park with Thorn until then."

"You're gonna *wait* all afternoon?"

"Yep."

She rolled her eyes. "Look, if you're willing to wait twenty minutes, I'll go with you guys."

First Thorn, now Aggie. Maybe the kids from Frazier Elementary wanted to come along, too.

I accepted the bag. "Don't worry about it—"

"Do you think I'm letting you go to another creepy shop without backup? I know Central Park better than you guys. Go have a seat over there next to the Thunderdome."

I eyed the table next to the nose-picker with distaste.

"Fine," she grumbled. "Go sit in the car with Thorn. I'll wrap up things, then I'll be out."

A half hour later, as promised, Aggie rushed out of Barney's. She hopped in with another bag of sandwiches while Thorn got comfortable in the back. I took over the driving.

Soon enough, I had the radio on and a somewhat construction-free drive up to New York City. The company was better too. After experiencing the joy of riding around with Rex last week, I welcomed hearing Aggie's loud smacks from eating her sandwich and Thorn's light snores from the backseat.

"Did you eat everything?" I asked her less than an hour into the trip.

"There's one left," she replied. "Make that half of one. There might be some chips left in the bag..."

"How generous of you."

"Just kidding. There's half a sandwich and a whole bag of chips." She turned up the air conditioning to full blast as we entered the Lincoln tunnel into Manhattan. "Last time you had to buy some creepy rattle. What do you have to buy this time?"

"The text said something about buying clothes from a mystical pop-up shop in Central Park."

"He probably wants you to buy him some lucky undies."

I shuddered. "Naw, he wants me to buy five shirts from a Yule Cat."

"What's that?"

"According to Icelandic folktales, the Jólakötturinn is this gigantic cat. During the Christmas season, those guys travel through the countryside looking for food. If kids come across them and they're not wearing new clothes, the Jólakötturinn eats them."

"That sounds so wrong."

"Pretty much, but we should be good since we're adults." I chuckled. "Well, I'm an adult. I don't know about you."

"Oh, stop it."

"You'll be fine." I paused a bit for dramatic effect. "Anybody who eats you is guaranteed to get indigestion."

Aggie flipped me off. "So we go to the park, find the pop-up shop, get the goods, then you're done, right?"

"That's it…I hope."

Forty minutes later, we left the car behind in a parking garage to walk to West 81st Street.

"What do you want to do while we wait?" Thorn asked. "Want to check out some shops?"

"I think I'll be good for the next century," I replied.

Thorn and Aggie exchanged a knowing look.

"Oh, stop you two," I said. "Let's walk around, have something to eat, and then we'll go to the park."

We spent the next three hours doing what Aggie called boring tourist stuff. We toured the American Museum of Natural History and raided the candy bins at the M&M'S store near Times Square. I truly believed our short trip beat fishing in Maine by a mile.

By the time the sun dipped low in the sky, we returned to the park entrance off West 81st Street. The soft breeze carried the scent of spring blossoms and the hum of city life.

"Please tell me Seamus gave you a clue," Aggie said with a sigh. "This park is huge."

"He said to check around Bank Rock Bay," I replied.

Aggie took in dusk's waning light. "I love this time of day," she whispered. "Even the ugliest street corner looks like a painting at sunset."

"It's beautiful, isn't it?" Thorn agreed.

I scanned the park, searching for the telltale signs of supernatural activity.

"Back when I was a kid," she added, "I loved how I could feel alone here, yet not be alone, if you know what I mean."

"That's New York for you," I whispered.

We headed into the park down 79th Street Traverse towards Bank Rock Bay. Night hadn't fallen yet and the park was full of visitors. Couples strolled hand in hand, whispering sweet nothings to each other, while runners dashed past us, their breaths ragged and their footsteps heavy on the pavement.

So far, I hadn't seen anything unusual.

We arrived at Bank Rock Bay, the water's surface shimmering in the fading light. In the distance, the skyline stood bright. We approached the edge of the pond and took in the small docks and scenic spots for tourists. Through the water's reflection, I caught the nearly full moon. In just two days, we'd feel the irresistible call to hunt.

Thorn suddenly tilted his head. "Do you hear that?" he asked, eyes narrowing. "It sounds like jingle bells, but...off-key."

I listened intently, and sure enough, I heard the peculiar melody. We followed the sound, rounding a corner and spotting a tall, gangly woman with curly black hair and unnaturally long fingernails. She stood on the opposite side of a bike with an overstuffed trailer attached.

"Do you think that's her?" Thorn asked.

"I think so," I replied.

The pale, dark-haired woman had to be the Yule Cat hiding behind a spell.

"Let's see how close we can get," Aggie suggested. "If she gobbles up a kid, you got the right person."

"Let's hope the cat doesn't do homicides in broad daylight." I headed over and Thorn kept up with me.

"Most New Yorkers do *everything* out in the open," Aggie said, bringing up the rear.

As we got closer, I could make out the Yule Cat and her belongings. She had a brand-new looking mountain bike painted midnight blue. The frame was adorned with intricate silver filigree that shimmered in the strange glow cast by the Christmas lights. Much to my amusement, the Yule Cat had filled the tiny trailer until the contraption defied the laws of physics. The olive-green tarp draped over the trailer bulged at the seams with bits of clothing poking out.

The off-key jingle bells continued to play as my target worked. The dark-haired woman unzipped the bag on the trailer and hung up garments on tree branches, her movements smooth and precise. She had shirts of all kinds for sale, from simple cotton tees to elaborate silk blouses with delicate embroidery.

With every item she hung, the Yule Cat added the scents of nutmeg and cinnamon. The air around the tree grew heavy with Christmas cheer and drew in the supernaturals.

"She's got clothes for sale," I whispered. "That's our girl."

As if on cue, wood nymphs dressed in casual clothing emerged from the forest, their curiosity piqued by the strange garments. They flitted between the branches, their delicate fingers sifting through the shirts and pants before approaching the woman.

"Excuse me," the wood nymph said. "I'm interested in this

sun dress, but I must say, the price is a bit high for the quality."

The Yule Cat's eyes formed slits. "What do you mean?"

"Well," the nymph replied, "these clothes are knock-offs. They smell *used*, too."

The Yule Cat frowned, her long fingernails tapping rhythmically against the handlebars of her bike. "Fine," she said, her voice a low growl as she fished through the trailer for something else. "How about this dress? Fifty bucks is a great deal for this one."

The wood nymph scoffed. "That could be as bad as the other one. I'll take it for thirty."

"These prices are a steal. Are you *really* going to haggle?"

"Is this new or has it been worn before?" she asked simply.

The Yule Cat's true form bristled under the glamour. "Be careful, my woodland sister."

"Let me have it for thirty-five and I'll pretend you didn't eat the last person who wore this..."

The Yule Cat hesitated, then with a dismissive wave of her hand she said, "Very well."

The wood nymph nodded, taking the sundress and disappearing behind a nearby tree to try it on. Moments later, she emerged, and the dress fit her perfectly.

"I must admit, it is lovely," the nymph said. "However, I still believe it's only worth twenty-five."

The Yule Cat kept her mouth shut as the victorious wood nymph handed the Yule Cat the cash.

"Damn shame she probably ate those people," Aggie said to me. "That black top is nice to be honest."

Thorn chuckled.

We hurried to draw closer. Once we passed a set of trees, we found the woman, her bike, and the clothes had disappeared. Even her music had cut off.

"Guess she sold everything?" Aggie remarked.

"I can still smell her," I said. "How did she disappear so fast?"

"Don't know, but she couldn't have gone far." Thorn searched the ground for tire tracks.

Around us, the park had become eerily silent, the once-lively atmosphere replaced by a heavy, unnerving stillness. We'd left the more scenic part of the pond and now stood among the trees lining the water.

"She can't have gone far," I said.

We spread out a bit and searched around. With each step, a familiar feeling, the same one I'd felt back at the lightning bird shop and The Bends parking lot came over me.

"I don't like this," Thorn said quietly. "We're being tracked."

Reluctantly, I told them about what I'd seen outside of Umbane's shop.

"Could it be Diana?" Thorn asked.

"I don't think so." I glanced around, seeing nothing amiss. Just some tourists on the other side of the ponds and a couple walking their collie down a well-lit trail.

"We should split up," Thorn suggested. "I'll draw whatever's following us away while you two look for the Yule Cat. I'll move faster in wolf form."

I hesitated but finally nodded. As we prepared to separate, Aggie joked, "Maybe she's off hunting for more clothes."

I scowled, not amused by Aggie's attempt at humor.

Thorn found some bushes and shifted. Aggie and I waited off to the side until he emerged not long after.

Moments later, Thorn disappeared to the east and we took off to the west.

"See anything?" I asked.

"Nothing."

Suddenly, a nearby human screamed before their shout was cut short.

"Oh shit," Aggie breathed.

Something came fast from the right. We sidestepped out of the way as the trees parted and a gigantic midnight black cat tore across the path. A dog-like beast the size of a truck bolted after the cat.

God help me, it was a hellhound.

The Yule Cat hissed and veered to the left, scampering over a bench and doubling back—right in our direction.

For half a second, we stared at it before Aggie pushed my back and we ran. The Yule Cat raced past us and darted to the left, leaping over a bike rack before she scampered up a huge tree.

The hellhound slammed into the tree and clawed at the trunk. It barked and snarled, flashing its dagger-like teeth. When the cat didn't come down, the hound rammed its head into trunk. The whole tree shook until the cat came crashing back down.

Aggie and I didn't get far before the cat zipped past us again. This time Thorn tore out of the woods, a blur of light-colored fur, to draw the beast away. The hellhound didn't take the bait and lunged at us. I ran faster, wishing I'd shifted like Thorn. The hound picked up the pace, and with one swipe, it flung Aggie across the lake. Her body rolled across the bank and disappeared into the bushes.

"Aggie!" I didn't have time to stand there long. The hellhound came at me and I chased after the cat. We ran deeper into the park. There were too many humans and not enough places to hide. I stuck to the woods and avoided the footpaths, but the hellhound was faster and caught up with the cat, snagging her long tail with its teeth. The hellhound yanked backward. The cat turned around with her claws extended and they collided with a thunderous boom. I tried to get away, but I couldn't avoid their rolling bodies as the hellhound snapped its jaws at the cat, seeking to sink its teeth into the cat's flesh. They crashed into trees, splintering the trunks and sending branches flying. I scrambled for a safe spot underneath a walking bridge, only for the hellhound to swipe at the Yule Cat and send her careening into the overpass. I rushed out from under the structure as their combined weight crushed the bridge.

The two creatures formed a crazy jumble of hissing and snarling and scratching. The hellhound was stronger, its powerful jaws finally clamping down on the cat's leg with a sickening crunch. The Yule Cat, however, was nimble and used her agile body to twist free from the hellhound's grip. After a deep hiss, she left deep gouges in the hellhound's jowls. The cat scampered to get away again, but the hellhound lunged, locking its jaws around the cat's neck. Without hesitation, I grabbed the nearest rock and threw it at the hound. The stone struck the dog's nose. The beast stalked in my direction then charged.

With the hound's attention diverted, the bleeding feline staggered away as I took off in the opposite direction. My breath came in short gasps as the hellhound tore through park benches, plowed past terrified humans, and bent iron fences in pursuit. I sprinted for a busy New York street. Cars and trucks roared down the road. Almost there. Maybe it wouldn't follow me—then I spotted a family of four in our path. Not good. I turned sharply to the right.

My turn slowed me down and the hellhound closed in. Its foul breath bathed my back with each pant.

The Yule Cat appeared out of nowhere, knocking me out of the hound's way. I rolled down a hill, only for her to swoop me up in her arms and make a run for it on two feet. She rushed for the nearest manhole, lifted the lid, and tossed me inside. I fell into the disgusting, unforgiving sewer. A much smaller Yule Cat raced in after me, not waiting a moment to reseal the lid and grab me again like a mother would hold a pup. In the dark, I couldn't see, but I felt the chilled water soaking through my clothes. The cat zipped through tunnel after tunnel, going left and right until we came to a stop at a junction point.

Gingerly, the cat released me and backed away. Light streaming through holes from a sewer lid above revealed the animal's bleeding leg.

"You're hurt." I approached the cat and she puffed up, her matted fur standing on end.

"I won't hurt you." I staggered back until I hit a gooey sewer wall. I cried out as if burned, then hurried without thinking over to the nearby ladder.

Somehow, the cat spoke. "Don't be foolish," she growled.

"But my mate and friend are out there. I need—"

"The hellhound has your scent now. Give it time to search elsewhere."

"A damn hellhound…" I collapsed against the ladder and gripped the rung hard.

"That was one of the pups." The cat stretched out her back and shuddered before she curled up. "You bear the huntress' mark," she added matter-of-factly.

"I know," I whispered, wishing I knew if Thorn and Aggie were okay. I climbed up a single rung, then another.

"Just a bit longer. It's almost left the park." The Yule Cat's green eyes slowly blinked at me. "Consider yourself lucky. The older ones don't give up as easily."

"Thanks." I chortled. The sound felt weird to my ears. Had I lost it already? "I was supposed to buy some shirts from you, and I drew that thing your way. I'm sorry."

The Yule Cat bared her teeth. "As much as I'd like to rip your head off, at least you intervened on my behalf." The cat licked its wound, and I gagged.

Oh heaven above, that's so nasty. All those germs. I couldn't shake the thought of millions of microorganisms screaming with glee as they stormed into our bodies. I opened and closed my fists until I could think straight.

"We're even now." The Yule Cat went quiet before it spoke again. "I shouldn't help you, but if you want those shirts, you'll find my bike chained up behind the boat landing."

"Thank you."

"If you're as enchanted as you appear to be, you'll find it." Then the cat disappeared down the sewer line. I didn't follow it.

Carefully, I made my way up the ladder. I listened for movement above and only heard the footsteps from nearby humans. Was it safe now? I waited two breaths before I lifted the lid and scampered out. An older man spotted me and gave me a wide berth.

The closest street sign read West 81st. At least I wasn't too far away. I ran back to the park, checking corner after corner for the hound. Half a block away, I turned a corner and found my beloved.

"Thorn." I ran into his arms and he enveloped me.

"Where have you been?" Then he sniffed. "Doesn't matter. You're safe."

"Have you seen Aggie?" I pulled back and checked on him. He didn't have so much as a scratch.

"She's hurt, but she's safe." He kept glancing around like I did. "I left her behind to find you."

We hurried back to the park.

"And the hound?" I asked.

"Gone," he replied bitterly. "Why did it wait until now to attack you?"

We darted past some street performers.

That was a good question, but then again, now that I'd

faced my foe, I knew the answer. "It's a pack predator—like us. I wouldn't attack without knowing my prey."

"So it waited," Thorn grumbled.

"And it assessed my weaknesses and *strengths*. Once it was confident, the hellhound made its move. Now, the endless chase begins."

CHAPTER TWENTY-TWO

As much as I wanted to take Aggie and run, Thorn told me to snag the clothes first.

"We're not leaving without those damn shirts," he grated out. Thorn ran with me until we spotted the Yule Cat's abandoned trailer.

As the creature had promised, I found the bike chained up outside of the Back Row Bay boat landing. My hands shook as I searched through the dresses and shirts. Would Seamus care what I bought? Should I get something for one of his *ladies?* I tried to fit my arm in one of the sleeves and it got stuck. Lovely. Every single piece was petite or a child's size.

I shook my head and moved quickly to grab five newish-looking T-shirts. Hope Seamus liked the color green, 'cause I'd seen enough red tonight to last a while.

After I grabbed the shirts, Thorn led me to Aggie and we found her prone form in the berry thickets. She moaned in pain when I touched her arm.

"We gotta go," I whispered as I ran my hands across her face.

My best friend grunted. Gently, I helped her sit up, careful to avoid the protrusions from broken ribs.

"Damn, that thing got you good," I said.

"That was a big ass dog," she said. "Wait, is it still around?"

"The Yule Cat said it left the park not too long ago, but if it's been tracking me hundreds of miles, then it will probably return."

She grimaced. "Wouldn't be hard to miss it."

"Not exactly. I saw it this morning. It can make itself invisible and change its size like the Yule Cat." I drew her arm around my shoulder to help her stand. "And that cat even said that thing is a *baby*."

"I bet its mom is one big *bitch*." She cackled at her horrible joke and held her side in pain.

"That's what you get."

"Speaking of *getting* something, did you get those shirts? This trip shouldn't be for nothing."

"Yeah, I got 'em."

"Good. 'Cause I think you got much bigger problems than Seamus now."

"My thoughts exactly."

~

Instead of heading home, Thorn hit the road. We drove three hours north into upstate New York before doubling back south to the Connecticut coast. We could've escaped to Canada, but I had business to settle.

Soon enough, we reached the ferry in Bridgeport and it was time for us to split up again. I'd meet the leprechaun while they took the long way home.

"Are you sure you don't want me to come with you?" Thorn asked.

"I'm sure. Just buy us some more time." Our kiss didn't

feel like the last one, so I got on the boat without reservations.

I didn't have to wait long, and the boat took off. Thorn waved from the shoreline. Without watching me depart, Aggie and Thorn drove north again to throw off the trail while I headed to Port Jefferson to the south.

I gripped the ferry railing and tried to rest, but my gaze kept skipping to the shore. The hellhound stalked out there, lurking out in the New York countryside. Apprehension sent a shudder through me. My hands grew numb, so I let go of the railing. The quiet conversation on the boat should've distracted me, but the wolf within clawed at my skin. *Run*, it urged. *Seek the safety of the woods.*

To still my rising fears, I scanned the faces of the few early morning passengers, and I adjusted the rucksack I carried. The silver hammer's handle poked my side, but I ignored it. At least the feather and the shirts were tucked away. Soon enough, I'd throw all this at the leprechaun.

As the ferry chugged toward Port Jefferson, I allowed myself to doze off, my grip on the pack never wavering. When I arrived at my next destination, I steeled myself for the walk ahead. It was rush hour and commuters filled New York City trains and subways. I joined the herd, a wolf hiding among the sheep. Two very long hours later, I reached O'Malley's Pawn and Jewelry in Brooklyn.

Once I walked in, I grimaced. His air conditioner was about to keel over. The rattling unit belted out lukewarm air and the trapped heat turned the shop into an oven. Didn't matter—I wasn't here to hang out. I found the leprechaun standing behind his bullet-proof glass at the other end of the shop, but he had customers this time, a leprechaun couple named Chair and Fianna. The pair argued and milled about in front of the questionable rings in the glass display.

Should I tell them those ruby rings would turn his lady

friend's fingers green? Nah, I'd let Seamus dig his own end-of-the rainbow hole.

I waved at Seamus, but his gaze was set on his indecisive customers. Couldn't he help me while they looked? I had a damn hellhound searching for me. I edged closer.

Cahir paced back and forth as he passionately argued his case. "Why do we have to go south for our honeymoon? Leenane is the *most* beautiful place in all of Ireland," he said. "They got plenty of pubs, friendly people." He gasped as if recalling a pleasant memory. "Kylemore Abbey, yes, that's the place. It's like something out of a storybook."

Fianna folded her arms. "Valentia Island has its own charm. The Fogher Cliffs are breathtaking, and my ma told me we'd have the best lovers' strolls."

I unzipped the rucksack, making sure the sound carried across the room. Neither noticed.

Cahir waved a dismissive hand. He'd yet to check out the rings. "But can you really compare a bunch of *boring* cliffs to Kylemore Abbey? They've got gardens, the reflection of the castle on the lake—that never gets old, I say."

As the leprechaun couple continued their discussion, I rolled my eyes and mumbled under my breath, "Not sure when you're gonna see all those sights with all that rain. Great for rainbows, I suppose."

Cahir overheard my comment. "Rain is a part of Ireland's charm. And I'll have you know that all that rainfall makes the most beautiful rainbows." He added, *"In Leenane."*

"Oh, Cahir, don't be ridiculous." Her voice rose in agitation. "Everyone knows that the rainbows on Valentia Island are the best."

I should have kept my mouth shut.

The couple continued their impassioned debate, each presenting the merits for their preferred location, but as the minutes dragged on and their voices grew louder, I considered tossing the bag's contents across the floor.

Finally, the couple exhausted their arguments, only to turn to me.

"What do you think?" Fianna asked. "Which one would you choose?"

I swallowed an impatient sigh. "Both places sound beautiful, but I really have more important things to worry about right now—like staying alive."

They blinked at me.

To fill the silence, I added, "Are you going to buy something? 'Cause I need a moment with Seamus." I placed the silver hammer on the counter next to the register, startling the couple and sending a ringing *clang* throughout the shop. On top of the hammer, I left the feather and shirts.

"Sorry for butting in like this, but I have a hellhound chasing me," I said stiffly.

Now it was the leprechaun couple who leaned away from *me* this time.

"Here's everything," I added. "As per our deal, I got this done within one month. Are we good?"

A sly grin spread across Seamus's face as he extended his hand. "We're good, lass. You held up your end of the bargain."

I regarded his outstretched hand and tried not to laugh. I nodded and left.

"Good luck to you," Seamus called out to my retreating back. "You're *gonna* need it and more."

CHAPTER TWENTY-THREE

Without fanfare, I journeyed home by myself. Since I didn't have a car, I took the jump point from Manhattan back to Jersey. Along the way, I checked behind each corner, almost expecting the Diana's hound to pop out with a wave and a tooth-baring snarl.

Once I trudged up to my house, I knew without a doubt that this place wasn't my home anymore.

Thorn had beat me back and had set his plan in motion. My heart sank to see his packed up SUV with an attached U-Haul.

The minute she shows up, we're out of here, Thorn had promised. While I'd delivered the goods, Thorn had started packing with Benny and Melvin's help.

As much as I wanted to say something, I staggered to the bathroom for a proper shower. I fumbled about the room, finding even trivial things like our toothbrushes were already stowed away. All Thorn had left in here was a sad sliver of soap and a fresh towel. Right now, I didn't need much more. An hour later, I emerged from the bathroom, ready for the next step.

I found Thorn in the kitchen packing up the utensils. "Are you heading into town?" he asked.

"Yeah, I need to speak to Bill."

He put down his box and drew me into his arms for a hug. "I just quit, too. It wasn't easy."

"It's not supposed to be, but I'm not safe here." I sighed. "Is Aggie okay?"

"I dropped her off at Brenna's place. The witch said she'd take care of her."

That was a relief. Brenna was a physician and she'd know what to do. There were so many people and things for me to worry about. "What about the bills? The house?"

"I got this, babe. We'll rent it out until we…figure things out." His voice trailed off.

"What time are we leaving?" I slipped my arms around his waist and clutched him tightly.

"We're outta here before sunset."

"And your dad?" There were so many little things. Too many that I hadn't thought about.

"He'll be fine. He has my brother and they'll watch over the pack while we're gone."

"You two are getting along better—"

"You act like I can't pick up a phone and call."

My throat dried up as my family's faces—from the scruffy to the rouged and smiling—flashed before my eyes. "For some families, a call isn't enough."

"No, it's not."

I wiped away the tears before grief could carry me away. "I'm exhausted, but I need to get over to The Bends before I chicken out."

"Let's go." He took my hand and we walked to my Altima.

The ride into South Toms River was silent. I took in the streets and shops, the familiar lines and curves a comfort. This place was my hometown. The place where I snuck out at night to meet with friends and where I watched Thorn from afar in high school. The thought of turning my back on my home and my pack tore at my stomach and left me weepy again.

Thorn intertwined his right hand with my left and squeezed. At least I wouldn't be alone. I'd never be alone again, but what state would I be in after we left?

Finally, we arrived at The Bends. My second home. The parking lot was nearly full. Somehow, I grabbed the handle and got out.

"I'm gonna park. Get in and get out," he said.

"Okay."

On the way inside, I passed Mrs. Weiss. The wind witch smiled, revealing her red lipstick-covered dentures. "Do you have anything good today?" she asked.

"We always do," I reassured her.

Another regular, Mrs. Kite, escaped the building with a huge grin. When she spotted me, she gave me a dirty look and marched over to her car.

"Thanks for coming!" I called after her.

I trudged around The Bends and slipped through the back doors. The moment I stepped into the office and found Bill working at his desk, I released a long sigh. I'd miss this place. The familiar scent of old books and worn leather filled the air, but I could hardly appreciate it now. It was time to tell Bill about my resignation, but the words were difficult to find.

Finally, Bill looked up from his computer, his piercing gaze meeting mine. "Thought you took the day off?" Then he added, "What's on your mind?"

Taking a deep breath, I blurted out, "It's time for me to go. Diana's hellhound is coming for me, and I can't put you or the store in danger."

Bill pulled off his glasses and rested them on the desk. For once, concern etched his pale features. "Where will you go?" he asked, his voice gruff but caring.

"I don't know yet," I admitted. "I just know I can't stay here."

"It's for the best." Bill nodded. "Keep your goblin blade close, and if you must, use Old Magic to protect yourself," he advised.

I returned his nod, knowing I couldn't avoid the powerful spells I'd learned forever. "I'll remember your advice, Bill. Thank you."

His expression softened, and he offered a rare smile. "Your job will always be here when you return. I don't trust anyone else with my business."

I tried to shrug off the compliment, knowing how seldom Bill offered praise. "I appreciate that," I said through a voice thick with emotion.

Bill got up and ventured out to the sales floor without saying goodbye. Didn't surprise me. He wasn't the type.

I grabbed a box from the back and packed up my desk. Once I was done, I stepped out of the antique store and into the parking lot. Thorn waited next to the car. Meanwhile, Rex approached me from under the awnings.

"I heard you're leaving." Rex still had a limp, but his condition had improved over the last couple of days.

"Yeah, it's for the best."

"Are you sure about that?"

I stared at him. "If I stay here, everyone around me will get hurt."

"And? The pack is stronger together than we are apart."

"My *problem*," I emphasized the word with a poke at my chest, "is bigger than what the pack can handle. It's even bigger than your ego."

That got a smile out of him, albeit brief.

"You're really good at your job, you know," he admitted.

I should buy a lottery ticket. Five of them. A compliment from Bill *and* Rex in one day.

He continued. "I absolutely hate you, but I respect your bravery. You got massive balls, Nat. Just wanted you to know that."

"Thanks, Rex. I appreciate your honesty, but next time you don't have to tell me you hate me." That last statement dripped with sarcasm, but I'd done what Dr. Frank had told me to do. I gave him a straightforward response.

Rex didn't look that torn up as I got in the car with Thorn. He shot Thorn a curt nod before we pulled away from the job that had lifted me out of the ashes and gave me purpose.

I hoped I could return someday.

CHAPTER 24

The drive home down the scenic Double Trouble State Road stretched out. Thorn remained silent in the driver's seat, his window rolled down and his arm stretched out to catch the breeze between his fingertips. My window was closed. The cool air fluttered against my face, but I couldn't push away the scent from wildflowers growing along the road, the sounds of robins and black skimmers. No matter how hard I tried to keep my gaze set on the road, my heart drifted to the forest.

My fists clenched. A part of me wanted to bolt. I'd jump out of the car and slip between the elm trees. Mother forest would welcome me. I'd run forever and draw the huntress away from my family.

Instead of reaching for the door, I grasped Thorn's right hand. He took the wheel with his left.

I waited for him to speak. He always had something soothing to say when my nerves were frayed. But he said nothing and merely smiled. He even leaned to the right so I could rest my head against his shoulder.

Two turns later, we reached the country road up to our cottage. I prepared myself to haul out the last of my belongings and leave my family behind.

And then I saw Uncle Boris.

He sat on top of Aunt Vera's minivan, his face pensive as he balanced a cig between his lips and fumbled the cords to tie down the cargo bag on top. Aunt Vera fussed at him in Russian as her two older teenagers watched videos on their phones from inside the van.

Right beside Aunt Vera's car, Aunt Olga spoke quietly with Mom and Dad. Their respective cars were filled to the brim. Grandma waved at me, even laughing when she caught what had to be my shocked expression.

"What's going on." My voice sounded hollow. "What are they doing?"

"Looks like we got company," Thorn said smoothly.

"Company?" I said. "Oh, no no. If those hellhounds come for me—"

"You won't be alone," he finished. "You'll never be alone again as long as you have your family."

"Thorn…" I twisted in the seat and gaped at my brother Alex and his wife Karey. Their little station wagon was tucked behind my parents' car. "How long have you been planning this?"

"When the nightmares kept coming, I'd had enough. After meeting with your parents, your grandma, and my dad, we came up with a plan." He chuckled as he got out. "Actually, this is all Farley's doing. He called in a favor with a mechanic to get everyone's cars road ready."

"That was generous of him." After everything I'd been through with Farley, I hadn't expected him to go above and beyond.

"Is he coming with us?" I asked, searching for him.

"No, he's staying behind with Will to take care of the pack."

"It would've been nice to see him before we left."

"That's not his thing. After Mom died, he never liked farewells. He just told me he was proud of me and to protect everyone."

"But I like goodbyes." Especially if I might not return…

Before I could fall into my dark thoughts, the Stravinsky clan swarmed us.

"I packed enough food for our first stop!" my mom declared proudly. "Thorn told me he got everything, but he forgot the sanitary products you left in the bathroom. I got those for you."

That got a laugh from me. Thorn rolled his eyes.

"Misha, do you have enough diapers for the baby?" Dad asked my brother.

"We're fine," Alex groaned. "You and mom bought too much."

"Oh, hush." Mom stole the toddler from Karey's arms and snuggled up on her grandbaby. My niece giggled. "I get to spend the summer with my darling."

"Should they be coming with us?" I asked my mom.

"We go where you go," Karey said firmly.

Alex added, "My wife told me her sisters in the forest will keep an eye out. Their communication network isn't as fast as a cell phone, but we should get a heads up if anyone sees a hellhound passing through their meadow."

"That's good to hear. So where are we going?" I asked.

Thorn had mentioned heading up to a cabin in Maine for a while. Now that we had more folks to take care of, I had no idea how we'd house all these people. Nervousness threatened to steal my breath, but Grandma took my hand.

"Remember that shop from my research?" she asked.

I nodded.

"We need to find it. A long time ago, your grandfather told me about a legend about shop in the great northern countryside to the west. I believe it's in Maine, but we'll need help to find it."

"Grandma," I replied, "we can't just drive around until we find a shop."

Aunt Vera and Mom made dismissive noises as if to say, "why can't we?"

"What else can you do?" Grandma wore a frown as she gestured around her.

"I should just disappear," I said. "You all should stay."

"No, *you* will listen." She even growled to make her point. "In that shop, we will come across a seed. We will bring that seed here to summon a champion. That champion will drive those hounds away."

So that was why Mom and Grandma went through all those books, but why bring everyone along? I could find this powerful shop on my own.

Thorn winked at me and patted me on the back. His expression flat out said: *What Grandma wants, Grandma gets.*

"Looks like we're heading to Maine!" Uncle Boris shouted to everyone. "Do we stop in Massachusetts or—"

"We're not going north," Dad said firmly. "Our enemy is in that direction. We go west and go around her."

"I say we keep driving until we see city lights," Uncle Boris suggested.

"We must go north," Grandma said firmly.

My father bowed his head. "We must do all this safely, Mama."

"Then we go around that she-devil," Grandma spat with fire in her tiny form. "We use the power of the pack. Send scouts to the west with Natalya's scent. They'll leave breadcrumbs for the hounds. The rest of us will go north to search for the shop."

With a plan set to find this great champion, we took off in a single caravan with Uncle Boris' radio belting out eighties hits. As the miles stretched out, I refused to look behind me. I feared that when I turned around, I'd see death staring back at me instead.

The End

PRAISE FOR SHAWNTELLE MADISON

A smart, sexy, rip-roaring good time!

Coveted is odd, funny, original and not at all what you'd expect. The writing is excellent, the characters come off so realistic they should have their own reality show, and the story is authentic and original.

Characters of all shapes, sizes and species abound in this new series from debut author Madison…How can you go wrong when your heroine is a werewolf with OCD? Madison tells her story with a lot of humor, and readers will be waiting with bated breath for her next story.

This is the start of a funny and touching new paranormal series, which may be dealing with supernatural creatures, but gives them all very human problems that make them very relatable. I loved this book and can't wait to see what's in store for Natalya next!

ALSO BY SHAWNTELLE MADISON

Coveted Series

Collected (Prequel Novella) #0.5

Coveted #1

Kept #2

Pocketed (Novella) #2.5

Compelled #3

Cursed (Collection of Short Stories)

Flea Market Magic Series

Thrift Store Trolls #1

Deceptive Dime Store Demons #2

Lowdown Pawn Shop Leprechauns #3

Ferocious Flea Market Dragons #4

Heroes Run in Packs Series

Hadley Werewolves

Windham Werewolves

McGinnis Werewolves

Urban Fantasy/Paranormal Romance

Bitter Disenchantment

Repossessed

Taming the Viking's Dragon

At Your Service Series

Bound to You

Surrender to You

ABOUT THE AUTHOR

Shawntelle Madison is a Web developer who loves to weave words as well as code. She'd be reluctant to admit it, but if pressed, she'd say that she covets and collects source code. After losing her first summer job detasseling corn, Madison performed various jobs, from fast-food clerk to grunt programmer to university webmaster. Writing eccentric characters is her favorite job of all. On any given day when she's not surgically attached to her computer, she can be found watching cheesy horror movies or the latest action-packed anime. Shawntelle Madison lives in Missouri with her husband and children.